2GB KI ZINDAGI

DATA KHATAM : DREAMS BAKI

PANKAJ GARG

To everyone who has ever felt lost in the digital noise, this is for you.
May you find your way back to what truly matters—real connections, genuine moments, and the courage to live authentically.
And to the next generation, remember: the likes may fade, but your true worth never will.

Contents

Contents

Foreword

In an age where our lives often fit into the storage of a smartphone, it's easy to forget that real connections, emotions, and experiences can't be captured in megabytes. 2GB ki Zindagi is the story of Aryan, a young influencer who discovers that while digital fame might fill his notifications, it can never fill the deeper void of genuine fulfillment.

This book is not just a critique of social media; it's a reminder that life is meant to be lived beyond the screen. Aryan's journey reflects the internal tug-of-war many of us face—balancing the allure of instant gratification with the longing for authentic, offline experiences. His story will resonate with anyone who has felt trapped in the endless scroll of digital life, and it offers hope for those looking to reconnect with their true selves.

As you read 2GB ki Zindagi, I hope you find the courage to unplug and live a life that's not confined to a file size.

Preface

The inspiration for 2GB ki Zindagi came from observing the world we live in—one where our lives, emotions, and even our self-worth seem to be increasingly tied to the digital space. Aryan's story is a reflection of the journey that many of us, especially the younger generation, are going through as we navigate the highs and lows of social media. In a time when validation is sought through likes, and success is measured in followers, it's easy to lose sight of what really matters.

This book explores the impact of living in a world that feels full, yet is often hollow. Aryan's experiences are fictional, but they're grounded in the realities we face daily—the pressures to maintain a perfect online persona, the allure of fame, and the inevitable burnout that comes with it. But more than that, it is a tale of rediscovery, a path toward understanding that real life—relationships, passions, and purpose—cannot be compressed into the 2GB of storage on our devices.

As you follow Aryan's journey, my hope is that you will reflect on your own life. We all need reminders that while the digital world may be fast and flashy, the true essence of life is found in the slower, deeper moments that aren't always captured by a camera.

This book is an invitation to unplug, even if just for a little while, and explore the richness of life beyond the screen.

Acknowledgements

Writing 2GB ki Zindagi has been a journey filled with reflection, learning, and growth, and I am deeply grateful to everyone who helped me along the way.

First and foremost, I want to thank my family, whose constant support and understanding gave me the time and space to write this story. Your love and encouragement were my guiding light throughout this project.

To my friends, who never failed to inspire me with real, offline conversations that sparked many of the ideas in this book—thank you for reminding me of the value of authentic human connection. You've been the heart of this story without even knowing it.

A special thanks to my teachers and mentors, who nurtured my creativity and passion for storytelling. Your guidance has been instrumental in shaping me as a writer.

To everyone who has ever felt overwhelmed by the digital world, this book is for you. Your experiences and struggles have given me the insight to write Aryan's story with honesty and empathy.

Lastly, to every reader of 2GB ki Zindagi—thank you for taking this journey with Aryan. I hope this story resonates with you and reminds you to find balance in your own life.

With gratitude,
Pankaj Garg

Prologue

The world we live in today moves at the speed of light. Notifications, status updates, likes, and shares have become the currency of our time. We're more connected than ever, yet, somehow, many of us feel more alone. 2GB ki Zindagi is the story of Aryan—a social media influencer who seemed to have it all. Fame, followers, the glamorous life that most people can only dream of. But beneath the surface, Aryan was trapped in a cycle of digital validation and superficiality, disconnected from the real world and from himself.

This is not just Aryan's story; it's the story of many of us. We've all felt the pressure to be constantly online, to present a perfect version of ourselves to the world. But in the rush to stay connected, we often lose touch with who we really are.

As Aryan embarks on a journey to reclaim his life, he confronts the highs and lows of a hyper-connected digital world. Through his struggles, failures, and triumphs, Aryan learns to redefine success, rediscover joy, and reconnect with his true self.

This book is a reminder that no matter how plugged in we are, there is a world beyond the screens—a world of real relationships, real passions, and real life. 2GB ki Zindagi is a celebration of that world and a reflection of the balance we all seek.

Welcome to Aryan's journey. May it inspire yours.

The Digital World

1

The Digital Dive: Aryan's World of Pixels and Posts

"You've got 10 new notifications," my phone chimed cheerfully, as if it hadn't already demanded my attention fifty times that morning. I was in the middle of brushing my teeth—one hand gripping the toothbrush, the other holding the phone. Multitasking, they call it. I call it the art of living a double life: one in the mirror, and one on the screen.

My name is Aryan, and I'm what people call an "influencer." It sounds glamorous, doesn't it? The word itself is a bit too serious for what I actually do, which is mainly trying to convince people that my life is more interesting than it actually is. And today, my mission was to post about a new brand of toothpaste. How thrilling.

But first, the morning routine. I scrolled through my notifications—likes, comments, shares. The usual dopamine hits. I knew the drill: respond to a few comments, like some posts, and drop a witty remark on a friend's photo. The algorithm demands it. You have to feed it if you want to stay relevant.

Once I'd done my obligatory social media rounds, I finally finished brushing my teeth. I stared at my reflection in the mirror—a half-awake guy with bedhead that could rival a bird's nest, toothpaste foam at the corners of his mouth, and a phone glued to his hand. This was the real Aryan, the one that nobody saw on Instagram.

"Looking good, man," I said to myself, with a sarcastic grin. I snapped a quick selfie, running a hand through my hair to tame the chaos. The plan was to slap on a filter, caption it with something deep like, "Rise and grind," and post it. But as I stared at the picture, something inside me felt... off.

Maybe it was the toothpaste brand deal looming over me, or maybe it was the fact that I was faking enthusiasm about something as mundane as brushing my teeth. Whatever it was, it made me pause for a second. But only for a second.

"Snap out of it, Aryan," I muttered, shaking off the weird feeling. The show must go on.

I headed to the living room, where my setup was waiting. A ring light, a tripod, and a carefully curated background. You wouldn't believe how many hours I'd spent arranging my bookshelves to look casually intellectual. And don't get me started on the number of houseplants I'd killed in my quest to create the perfect 'natural' vibe.

As I set up the shot, I could hear my mom in the kitchen, clattering pots and pans. "Aryan, did you eat breakfast?" she yelled.

"Uh, not yet, Mom!" I called back, but my mind was already on the post. Breakfast could wait. The perfect post couldn't.

I squirted a generous amount of toothpaste onto my toothbrush, making sure to hold it up to the camera just right. "Hey guys, welcome back to my channel!" I started, my voice chipper and bright. "Today, I'm super excited to share with you this amazing new toothpaste that's going to change your morning routine!"

A little exaggerated? Maybe. But exaggeration was the name of the game.

I went on about the toothpaste's minty freshness, its whitening power, and how it would make your smile dazzle like a movie star's. I even threw in a few cheesy jokes for good measure. As I wrapped up the video, I flashed what I hoped was a convincing grin and hit the stop button.

And that was it. Another day, another post. I should have felt accomplished, but instead, that same weird feeling from earlier crept back. The feeling that I was more actor than influencer, playing a role that wasn't really mine.

I shrugged it off and started editing the video. That's when my phone buzzed again, this time with a message from my best friend, Ravi.

"Dude, you free tonight? Let's grab dinner."

Dinner with Ravi sounded great, but my calendar was packed with content creation. "Maybe another time," I typed back, but before I could hit send, I paused.

I missed hanging out with Ravi. We used to spend hours just talking and laughing about stupid things. But ever since I became "Aryan the Influencer," our hangouts had become less frequent, replaced by my obsession with likes and followers.

I deleted the message and typed, "Sure, let's do it," instead.

That night, as we sat in a small, cozy restaurant, eating pizza and laughing about old times, I realized how much I'd missed just being Aryan. Not the influencer, not the brand ambassador—just Aryan, the guy who loved pizza, bad jokes, and hanging out with his best friend.

"So, how's the influencer life treating you?" Ravi asked, a smirk on his face.

I chuckled. "It's… something, alright."

"Still selling toothpaste?" he teased.

"Yeah," I laughed, "and all sorts of other thrilling products. But honestly, it's not as glamorous as it looks."

Ravi nodded, his expression turning serious. "You know, you don't have to do this forever. There's more to life than followers and brand deals."

His words struck a chord. Deep down, I knew he was right. But the thought of stepping away from it all was terrifying. What would I do? Who would I be without my online persona?

"Maybe," I said, shrugging. "But for now, it's what I do."

We spent the rest of the evening joking and reminiscing, and for a few hours, I forgot all about likes, followers, and brand deals. It was just me and my best friend, laughing about the stupidest things, like we used to.

As I headed home that night, I couldn't shake Ravi's words from my mind. There was more to life than followers and brand deals. But what did that mean for me? I didn't have an answer yet, but for the first time in a long time, I felt like maybe—just maybe—I was ready to find out.

2
Digital Obsession

The first thing I did when I woke up was reach for my phone. Before my eyes had even fully adjusted to the light, I was already scrolling through notifications, checking for new comments, likes, and follows. It had become a ritual, one that I followed religiously every morning.

The numbers were all that mattered—the constant rise in followers, the influx of likes, the validation that came with every positive comment. My mind was consumed by the metrics, a relentless drive to keep growing, to stay relevant. The idea of taking a break, of disconnecting even for a moment, was unthinkable. I was always on, always available, always thinking about the next post, the next trend, the next opportunity to engage with my audience.

I spent hours crafting the perfect images. Whether it was a casual selfie, a candid shot, or a carefully staged scene, every post had to be just right. The lighting, the angle, the caption—it all had to be meticulously planned. I had learned the hard way that even the smallest mistake could lead to a dip in engagement, and I couldn't afford that.

Social media wasn't just a platform for me; it was my life. It dictated my schedule, my interactions, my thoughts. Everything revolved around my online presence. I was constantly glued to my phone, responding to comments, interacting with followers, and monitoring my feed to stay on top of the latest trends. It was exhausting, but I couldn't stop. The fear of losing my status, of becoming irrelevant, kept me going.

As I navigated through my day, my mind was always half in the digital world. Even when I was physically present, part of me was somewhere else, thinking about what I could post next or how I could tweak my content to get more engagement. I had become so engrossed in my online persona that I started to lose sight of who I was outside of it.

Lunch with friends turned into photo ops, with every meal needing to be documented and shared with my followers. Outings were planned not for fun but for the potential content they could produce. Conversations were peppered with thoughts about how something could be turned into a story or post. My friends would often joke that I was more interested in my phone than in them, and they weren't entirely wrong. But I couldn't help it; I was addicted.

The constant need for validation began to take its toll. Every time I saw a drop in followers or received a critical comment, it felt like a punch to the gut. I'd spend hours analyzing what went wrong, how I could have done better, what I needed to change. The pressure was suffocating, but the thought of stepping back, of losing everything I had built, was even more terrifying.

I had to be perfect, or at least appear to be. There was no room for flaws or mistakes. My online persona had become a carefully curated version of myself—one that was always happy, always on top of things, always successful. But the truth was far from that. Beneath the surface, the cracks were starting to show, and I was struggling to keep up the facade.

I knew I was obsessed, but I didn't know how to stop. Social media had become more than just a tool; it had become a part of me, a part that I couldn't imagine living without. But as the days went on, the weight of it all began to press down on me, and I started to wonder how much longer I could keep it up.

3

The Glamor of Influence

Every weekend, it was something new. A launch party for a brand, a rooftop event with a view of the city skyline, a collaboration shoot with another influencer. The invitations never stopped coming, and neither did the opportunities to show off the life everyone thought I had. From the outside, it looked like I was living the dream. My feed was filled with pictures of me dressed to the nines, clinking glasses with other social media stars, or lounging in some luxurious setting that most people could only dream of visiting.

But the truth was, I was exhausted.

The events were glamorous, sure, but they were also endless. Each one required me to be "on"—smiling, networking, making sure that every photo taken of me was perfect. The parties that people envied weren't really parties at all. They were work. They were opportunities to be seen, to be photographed, to be tagged by the right people, and to keep the followers coming. The glamorous outfits, the luxury settings, the carefully curated moments—all of it was for the content. None of it felt real.

And then there were the collaborations. On the surface, working with other influencers seemed like a dream come true. We'd meet in some trendy café or picturesque location, snap a few pictures together, and post them with captions that screamed #friendshipgoals. But the reality was far less glamorous. These collaborations were business transactions, plain and simple. We weren't friends; we were colleagues, each looking to benefit from the other's following.

As I smiled for yet another photo, surrounded by people I barely knew, I started to feel a gnawing emptiness. The more followers I gained, the more parties I attended, the more collaborations I did, the more I began to realize that my life was beginning to feel like one long performance. And the audience? They saw what I wanted them to see—the clothes, the parties, the smiling faces. But that was all it was: a performance.

After every event, I would come home to a quiet, empty apartment. I would sit on my couch, still in my designer clothes, and scroll through the photos from the night. I'd pick the best ones, edit them to perfection, and post them with just the right caption. The likes and comments would start pouring in almost immediately, but they didn't bring the satisfaction they once did. The praise and adoration that I had once craved now felt hollow.

There were moments when I would look at the photos I posted and feel a disconnect, like I was looking at someone else's life. The person in those pictures looked happy, confident, like they had it all. But deep down, I knew that wasn't the whole truth. My happiness was fleeting, dependent on the approval of people I didn't even know.

It was a strange dichotomy—being surrounded by people all the time, yet feeling so incredibly alone. The superficiality of it all started to wear on me. The endless cycle of praise and adoration, the constant need to be seen, to be liked, to be relevant—it was exhausting. And as I sat in my apartment, scrolling through the comments and trying to convince myself that it was all worth it, I couldn't shake the feeling that something was missing.

But what? I had everything I thought I wanted—fame, success, a life that others envied. Yet the more I achieved, the emptier I felt. The parties, the collaborations, the glamour—it all felt like a façade, and I was starting to realize that the life I had built wasn't bringing me the happiness I had hoped for.

For the first time, I began to question the path I was on. Was this really what I wanted? Was this what happiness looked like? I didn't have the answers, but I knew that the life I was living wasn't sustainable. Something had to change, but I didn't know what or how. All I knew was that the endless cycle of glamour and influence was leaving me feeling more empty and isolated than ever before.

4

The Pressure of Perfection

Every day started the same way. I'd wake up, check my phone, and immediately be hit with a flood of notifications. Comments, likes, messages—it was endless. And before I even got out of bed, I was already thinking about what I needed to do to maintain my image. The pressure was always there, lingering in the back of my mind like a shadow I couldn't shake.

Maintaining a perfect image wasn't just a job; it was an obsession. Every post had to be flawless, every caption had to be just the right mix of witty and engaging, every photo had to be meticulously edited until it looked like something straight out of a magazine. I'd spend hours on my phone, scrolling through my feed, analyzing what other influencers were doing, trying to figure out how I could do it better.

The pressure to outdo myself and others was relentless. It wasn't enough to simply post a good photo anymore. It had to be the best photo, with the best caption, posted at the best time to maximize engagement. I became a slave to the metrics, constantly refreshing my page to see how many likes I was getting, how many comments, how many shares. The numbers became an obsession, a way to measure my worth, my success, my relevance.

But the pressure didn't stop there. I wasn't just competing with others; I was competing with myself. Every post had to be better than the last. If one photo got a lot of likes, then the next one had to get even more. If a caption went viral, then the next one had to be even more clever, more relatable, more shareable. The fear of losing followers, of falling behind, of becoming irrelevant, was always there, gnawing at me.

And then there was the editing. Oh, the editing. It was a full-time job in itself. I'd spend hours tweaking every little detail of a photo—brightening the colors, smoothing out imperfections, adjusting the lighting—until it was perfect. But even then, I wasn't satisfied. I'd go back and tweak it some more, constantly second-guessing myself, wondering if it was good enough, if it would get the reaction I wanted.

The worst part was the captions. They seemed so simple, just a few lines of text, but they were the bane of my existence. Crafting the perfect caption was an art form. It had to be short but impactful, funny but not too forced, relatable but still unique. I'd write and rewrite the same caption over and over, agonizing over every word, every emoji, every hashtag. And even after all that, I'd still worry that it wasn't good enough.

But the pressure didn't just come from within. It came from everywhere. My followers had expectations, and I had to meet them. They expected perfection, and I couldn't let them down. If I posted something that wasn't up to their standards, they let me know. The comments would start pouring in, pointing out every flaw, every mistake. It was brutal, and it only made the pressure worse.

The fear of negative feedback was always there, lurking in the back of my mind. What if they didn't like it? What if they unfollowed me? What if my engagement dropped? The what-ifs were endless, and they kept me on edge, constantly striving for perfection, constantly pushing myself to do better, to be better.

But no matter how hard I tried, it was never enough. There was always something more I could do, something I could improve, something I could perfect. The pressure was suffocating, and it was taking a toll on me. I was exhausted, mentally and physically. The endless pursuit of perfection was wearing me down, but I didn't know how to stop. I didn't know how to let go.

The pressure to be perfect, to maintain this flawless image, was consuming me. It was all I thought about, all I cared about. My life had become a series of perfectly curated moments, each one carefully crafted to meet the expectations of my followers, to keep them engaged, to keep them liking, commenting, and sharing. But the more I tried to be perfect, the more I realized how imperfect it all was. The perfect life I had built was nothing more than a façade, and the cracks were starting to show.

5

A Lonely Success

Success has a strange way of isolating you. As my follower count grew and the brand deals rolled in, I found myself surrounded by people, yet somehow feeling more alone than ever. My life was full of parties, collaborations, and constant interactions, but there was an emptiness that I couldn't shake. The loneliness crept in slowly, at first just a whisper in the back of my mind, but it grew louder with each passing day.

On the surface, everything looked perfect. I was living the dream, or at least that's what everyone thought. I had the fame, the money, the admiration of thousands. People wanted to be around me, to be seen with me, to share in my success. But as my world expanded, the connections I had with others became increasingly superficial.

I had friends, or at least people who called themselves my friends. But the truth was, our relationships were transactional, built on mutual benefit rather than genuine connection. We bonded over photo ops and follower counts, brand deals and sponsorships, but beneath the surface, there was nothing real. Our conversations were shallow, revolving around the next big event or the latest trend, but never touching on anything of substance.

It was like we were all actors in a play, each of us performing our roles, but never really knowing the person behind the mask. We smiled for the cameras, laughed at the right moments, and played our parts to perfection, but when the cameras were off, there was an uncomfortable silence, a void that none of us knew how to fill.

I remember one night, sitting in the VIP section of a trendy club, surrounded by people who were supposed to be my friends. The music was loud, the lights were blinding, and the drinks kept coming, but I felt completely disconnected. Everyone around me was laughing, dancing, taking selfies, but I couldn't shake the feeling that I didn't belong there. It was like I was watching my life from the outside, a spectator in my own story.

I realized then that I had no one I could truly confide in. No one who really knew me, the real me. My online persona had taken over my life, leaving little room for anything real or meaningful. I had spent so much time crafting this perfect image, this larger-than-life persona, that I had lost touch with who I really was. The people around me only knew the version of me that I presented to the world, not the person I was inside.

It wasn't that I didn't want real connections. I craved them, more than anything. But I didn't know how to form them anymore. The lines between my real self and my online persona had blurred to the point where I wasn't sure who I was without the filters, the captions, the perfectly posed photos. I had built my life around this image, and it had taken over everything.

The loneliness was suffocating. I could be in a room full of people and still feel completely alone. The constant attention, the endless stream of messages, the constant validation from strangers—it all felt hollow. It was like eating junk food; it satisfied a craving in the moment, but left me feeling empty and unsatisfied.

There were times when I would scroll through my phone, looking at the thousands of messages and comments, and feel nothing. The praise, the admiration, the adoration—it all blurred together, losing its meaning. I had everything I had ever wanted, but I felt more alone than ever. The success I had worked so hard for had come at a cost, and I was starting to realize just how high that cost was.

I began to wonder if it was all worth it. The fame, the fortune, the attention—what was the point if it left me feeling so empty? I had traded real connections for superficial ones, and I was paying the price. The people around me were there for the perks, the parties, the Instagrammable moments, but when it came down to it, I was alone.

The loneliness wasn't just a feeling; it was a constant presence in my life. It followed me everywhere, a shadow I couldn't escape. I would wake up in the morning, check my phone, and feel the weight of it pressing down on me. I would go to events, smile for the cameras, and feel it gnawing at the edges of my mind. I would lie in bed at night, scrolling through my feed, and feel it settle in my chest, a dull ache that wouldn't go away.

I had achieved everything I had ever dreamed of, but it hadn't brought me the happiness I thought it would. Instead, it had left me isolated, disconnected, and profoundly lonely. I was surrounded by people, but I had never felt more alone.

6

Memory Trigger

It was an ordinary day, or at least it started out that way. I was in my usual routine—scrolling through social media, responding to comments, and planning my next post. The endless cycle of content creation and engagement had become second nature to me, a constant loop that I rarely broke free from. But that day, something unexpected happened. I received a message that would change everything.

It was from an unknown account, someone I didn't recognize, with no profile picture and no posts. Normally, I would have dismissed it as spam, but something about the message caught my eye. It was short, just one simple question: "Do you remember who you were before all this?"

At first, I was confused. What did they mean? Before what? But as I read the message again, something stirred inside me. A memory, a feeling, something I hadn't thought about in a long time. It was like a small crack in a dam, and suddenly, the memories started flooding back.

Before all this, before the followers, the fame, the brand deals—I was just Aryan. I was a guy who loved photography, who spent hours wandering around the city capturing the world through my lens. I was someone who found joy in the simple things, like a perfectly framed shot, a conversation with a friend, or a quiet moment alone with my thoughts.

Back then, life was different. It was simpler, more fulfilling in a way that had nothing to do with likes or comments or follower counts. I wasn't always thinking about how to curate my life for public consumption. I wasn't constantly analyzing my worth based on metrics and algorithms. I was just living, experiencing the world in a way that felt authentic and true.

As I sat there, staring at the message, I realized how much I had changed. My life now was a far cry from what it used to be. The things that once brought me joy had been replaced by the relentless pursuit of validation from strangers. I had traded the simplicity and contentment of my old life for the fleeting highs and crushing lows of social media fame.

The message kept playing over and over in my mind. "Do you remember who you were before all this?" It was a question I hadn't asked myself in a long time, and the more I thought about it, the more I realized I didn't have an answer. I had become so consumed by my online persona, by the need to maintain this image, that I had lost touch with who I really was.

The memories that surfaced were bittersweet. I remembered the days when I would spend hours in a coffee shop, editing photos not for the likes but for the love of the craft. I remembered the late-night conversations with friends, the kind where you lose track of time because you're so engrossed in the moment. I remembered the feeling of satisfaction that came from creating something meaningful, something that wasn't just a tool for engagement but a true expression of myself.

But those days felt like a lifetime ago. Somewhere along the way, I had gotten caught up in the race for more—more followers, more likes, more fame—and I had lost sight of the things that really mattered. The message had triggered something in me, a longing for the life I used to have, for the person I used to be.

I couldn't shake the feeling that something was missing from my life. Despite all the success, all the recognition, there was a void inside me that no amount of likes or followers could fill. I had built my life around this digital persona, but in doing so, I had lost touch with the person behind the screen.

The question haunted me. "Do you remember who you were before all this?" It was a reminder of a time when life was different, when my happiness wasn't tied to numbers on a screen, when I lived for the joy of the moment rather than the approval of others. It was a wake-up call, a jolt that made me realize how far I had strayed from the path I once walked.

That night, as I lay in bed, I couldn't stop thinking about the message. Who had sent it? And why? But more than that, I couldn't stop thinking about the memories it had stirred. The person I used to be, the life I used to live—it all seemed so distant, yet so close, like a dream I had just woken up from but couldn't quite remember.

For the first time in a long time, I felt a spark of something real, something genuine. It was a small spark, but it was enough to make me question everything. Was this really the life I wanted? Was this digital world worth the sacrifice of my true self? The questions swirled in my mind, and I knew I couldn't ignore them any longer.

Something was missing from my life, and I knew I had to find it. But to do that, I had to start by answering the question that had triggered it all: "Do you remember who you were before all this?"

7
Doubt Creeps In

The message had done more than just trigger memories—it had planted a seed of doubt in my mind. For the first time in what felt like forever, I found myself questioning the life I was living. As I went about my daily routine, I couldn't shake the nagging feeling that something was off, that maybe everything I had worked so hard to build was not as fulfilling as I had once believed.

It wasn't that I didn't enjoy the perks of my digital life. The fame, the recognition, the opportunities—it was all more than I had ever dreamed of. But beneath the surface, a creeping doubt had begun to take hold. Was this really what I wanted? Was this endless pursuit of likes and followers truly making me happy, or was it all just a facade?

Every time I posted a new photo, I felt a surge of excitement as the likes started rolling in. But that excitement was fleeting, quickly replaced by anxiety—Would this post perform as well as the last one? What if my followers didn't like it? What if I started losing followers? The constant need for validation was exhausting, and it left me feeling more drained than fulfilled.

The more I thought about it, the more I realized how much my self-worth had become tied to my online presence. Every comment, every share, every follower count had become a measure of my value. And the pressure to maintain that value was immense. I had built my life around this digital persona, but now I was starting to wonder if it was all an illusion.

I found myself thinking back to the message: "Do you remember who you were before all this?" The words echoed in my mind, each time stirring up more doubt. Before all this, I had dreams, passions, and a sense of purpose that wasn't dependent on external validation. But somewhere along the way, I had lost sight of those things, and now I was left questioning what my life had become.

The doubt grew stronger with each passing day. I started to see cracks in the facade I had carefully constructed. The glamorous events, the endless stream of content, the constant engagement—it all started to feel hollow, like a game I was playing for the sake of others, not for myself. I began to wonder if the life I was living was truly my own, or if I was just performing a role, a character in a story that wasn't really mine.

But even as these doubts took root, the thought of stepping away from it all terrified me. What would happen if I lost everything I had worked so hard to build? The followers, the fame, the opportunities—could I really just walk away from it all? The idea seemed impossible, like throwing away everything I had ever known.

The fear of losing it all was paralyzing. I had invested so much of myself into this digital world that the thought of leaving it behind felt like losing a part of myself. Who would I be without my followers, without the constant validation? Would I still matter? Would anyone care?

The doubt gnawed at me, but so did the fear. I was stuck in a limbo, torn between the life I had built and the life I had lost. The more I questioned my digital life, the more I realized how much of it was driven by fear—fear of losing relevance, fear of being forgotten, fear of not being enough.

I couldn't deny that the doubt was there, but I also couldn't bring myself to act on it. The spotlight was addictive, and the thought of stepping out of it was terrifying. I had worked too hard, sacrificed too much to just walk away. But deep down, I knew that something had to change. I couldn't keep living a life that felt increasingly disconnected from who I truly was.

The doubts were like whispers in the back of my mind, growing louder with each passing day. They made me question everything—my motives, my choices, my happiness. And while the fear of losing it all was still there, so was the desire for something more, something real.

I didn't have all the answers, and I didn't know what the future held. But one thing was certain—the doubt wasn't going away. It was there, a constant reminder that maybe, just maybe, the life I was living wasn't the life I truly wanted.

And so, the internal struggle began. I was at a crossroads, torn between the comfort of the familiar and the uncertainty of the unknown. The road ahead was unclear, but one thing was becoming increasingly certain—I couldn't ignore the doubt any longer.

8
The Strain of Duality

Living a double life was more exhausting than I had ever imagined. On one side, there was Aryan—the influencer, the social media star with a carefully curated feed, the life that everyone envied. On the other side, there was the real me—the person who once found joy in simple moments, who valued genuine connections, and who now felt increasingly lost in the digital whirlwind I had created.

Every morning, I would wake up and switch hats. The first part of my day was dedicated to maintaining my online persona. I'd meticulously plan my outfits, scout locations for the perfect backdrop, and brainstorm captions that would resonate with my audience. It was a routine that had become second nature, a necessary part of my existence. But beneath the surface, a growing sense of dissonance gnawed at me. The more I invested in my online life, the less connected I felt to who I truly was.

The duality of my existence was becoming unbearable. At events, I had to embody the confident, carefree Aryan that my followers saw. I smiled, laughed, and interacted in ways that felt forced, all for the sake of capturing the perfect moment. But when the cameras were off and the lights dimmed, I was left with a heavy sense of emptiness. The stark contrast between my online persona and my true self was widening, creating a chasm that I struggled to bridge.

I started to feel like I was living two separate lives—one online and one offline—and neither felt authentic. The online Aryan was everything I wasn't: effortlessly happy, perpetually busy, and always in control. The offline Aryan was struggling, grappling with loneliness, anxiety, and a deep sense of disconnection. Balancing these two identities required a constant performance, leaving me mentally and emotionally drained.

The strain of maintaining this duality began to seep into every aspect of my life. My relationships suffered as I became more preoccupied with my online presence. Friends noticed that I was always distracted, my attention divided between the real conversations we were having and the notifications on my phone. I found it difficult to be present, to engage authentically, because a part of me was always calculating the next post, the next engagement spike.

Even my personal space felt invaded by this duality. My apartment, once a sanctuary, was now a staging ground for my online persona. Every corner was meticulously arranged for photoshoots, every piece of decor chosen for its Instagrammable potential. It was as if I had transformed my living space into a set, sacrificing comfort and authenticity for the sake of appearances.

The more I tried to keep up with both lives, the more they began to clash. The online Aryan thrived on constant interaction, always seeking the next big thing, while the offline Aryan craved solitude, genuine connections, and a break from the relentless pace. This internal conflict created a persistent state of tension, a tug-of-war between who I was and who I was expected to be.

Sleep became elusive as my mind raced between these two worlds. I would lie in bed, my phone perpetually within reach, caught between the desire to disconnect and the fear of missing out. The boundary between day and night blurred, as my online life bled into my personal time. I found myself scrolling through my feed late into the night, unable to shut off the constant need for validation and connection.

My mental health began to decline under the weight of this dual existence. Anxiety and stress became constant companions, and the lines between reality and the digital facade I maintained started to blur. I struggled to remember what it felt like to simply be, without the pressure to perform or the need to present a flawless image to the world. The duality was not just a balancing act; it was a battle for my identity, a fight to reclaim the parts of myself that had been overshadowed by the demands of my online life.

I began to notice the subtle changes in myself—the way my laughter felt forced, the way my interactions lacked genuine emotion, the way I no longer recognized the person staring back at me in the mirror. The strain of living two lives was taking its toll, and I could no longer ignore the growing disconnect between my online persona and my true self.

One evening, after another exhausting day of events and endless content creation, I found myself alone in my apartment, surrounded by the very things that were supposed to represent my success. The facade felt hollow, the perfection unattainable, and the duality unsustainable. I sat on my couch, the weight of my dual existence pressing down on me, and realized that something had to change.

The duality had become too much to handle. I was caught in a cycle that left me feeling more lost and disconnected than ever before. The life I had built online was no longer a source of pride or joy, but a constant reminder of what I had sacrificed in the pursuit of fame. The strain of living two lives was too heavy a burden, and I knew that continuing down this path was leading me further away from the person I wanted to be.

In that moment of clarity, I began to understand that the only way to find true fulfillment was to reconcile these two sides of myself. It wouldn't be easy, and the path ahead was uncertain, but the strain of duality had shown me that something had to give. The digital world had consumed so much of me, but perhaps it was time to rediscover the parts of myself that had been buried beneath the layers of likes, followers, and curated content.

9
The Cracks Appear

The cracks in my carefully constructed world began to show in ways that I couldn't ignore. What had once been a seamless operation—a steady stream of content, a growing follower count, a flawless online presence—started to unravel at the seams. I had built my entire identity on this digital platform, and now, it was slipping through my fingers.

It started with small mistakes, things I wouldn't have missed in the past. I posted a photo without double-checking the edits, only to realize later that it wasn't up to my usual standard. The lighting was off, the angle unflattering, and the comments reflected the oversight. "Is everything okay, Aryan? This isn't like you." "What happened to your usual quality?" Each notification was a jab at my already fraying nerves.

The mistakes snowballed from there. I missed a deadline for a brand collaboration, something I had never done before. The email from the brand's representative was curt, a clear indication of their disappointment. I could feel the pressure mounting, and the more I tried to fix things, the more they seemed to fall apart. My once-perfect image, the one I had worked so hard to create, was beginning to show signs of wear.

Followers started to drop off, slowly at first, and then more noticeably. I would refresh my feed, hoping to see the numbers climb, but instead, I watched them dip. The comments and messages that had once been filled with admiration and praise now had an undercurrent of concern and critique. "You're not posting as much, Aryan. Everything okay?" "This content feels different. Are you losing your touch?" Each remark felt like a confirmation of my deepest fear—that I was losing control.

Panic set in as I realized the gravity of the situation. My sense of identity had become so intertwined with my online persona that I couldn't separate the two. The cracks in my digital facade weren't just superficial; they were deep fissures that threatened to swallow me whole. I had built my life around the idea of perfection, and now that perfection was crumbling.

I found myself obsessing over the numbers, refreshing my analytics page every few minutes, desperate for a sign that things were turning around. But the numbers didn't lie. Engagement was down, reach was shrinking, and the once-steady stream of brand deals began to slow. It was as if the entire foundation of my success was being eroded, bit by bit.

The stress of it all became overwhelming. I was constantly on edge, snapping at the few people still close to me, unable to focus on anything other than the impending sense of doom. My sleep, already restless, became practically nonexistent. I would lie awake at night, staring at the ceiling, my mind racing through a thousand scenarios, each one worse than the last.

In my desperation to regain control, I started to second-guess everything I did. Should I post more? Should I change my content style? Should I take a break and come back stronger? But every decision felt like a gamble, and the stakes were my entire identity. The more I tried to tighten my grip, the more things seemed to slip away.

The panic was palpable. I could feel it in the pit of my stomach, a constant churn that left me nauseous and exhausted. I had once thrived on the adrenaline rush of being in the spotlight, but now that same spotlight felt harsh and unforgiving. I was no longer in control of my narrative; it was controlling me.

The cracks in my image mirrored the cracks in my sense of self. I had invested so much of myself into this online persona that I no longer knew who I was without it. The person behind the screen, the real Aryan, was buried beneath layers of filters, captions, and likes. As my digital world began to fall apart, I realized how much of my self-worth had been tied to the approval of others.

It was a vicious cycle— the more I panicked, the more mistakes I made, and the more mistakes I made, the more I panicked. My mind was in a constant state of overdrive, running through endless what-ifs and worst-case scenarios. What if I lost everything? What if the followers never came back? What if this was the beginning of the end?

For the first time, I felt like I was truly losing control, not just of my online presence, but of my life. The cracks were no longer just surface-level; they were deep, and they were spreading. The image I had spent years crafting was shattering, and with it, my sense of who I was.

The realization that I was losing control was terrifying. It was as if I was standing on the edge of a cliff, the ground crumbling beneath my feet, and I had no idea how to stop the fall. The pressure and stress were too much to bear, and I was caught in a downward spiral that I didn't know how to escape.

The cracks had appeared, and they were impossible to ignore. I was no longer the flawless, unshakable Aryan that the world saw. I was a person on the verge of collapse, struggling to hold onto an identity that was slipping away. And as the panic set in, I knew that something had to change, or I would lose everything.

10

First Glimpse of Change

There's a saying that the most difficult step in any journey is the first one. For me, that step came in the form of a late-night message to someone I hadn't spoken to in years—my old friend, Rohan. He was someone who knew me long before the fame, before the followers, before the pressure to maintain a perfect image took over my life. I hesitated as I typed out the message, unsure of what to say or how he would respond. But I was desperate, and something told me that Rohan might be the lifeline I needed.

"Hey, it's been a while. Can we talk?" That's all I managed to send. I stared at the screen, waiting for the three little dots that would indicate he was typing back. Minutes felt like hours, and I could feel my heart pounding in my chest. Finally, a reply came.

"Of course. What's up?"

It was simple, unassuming, and it reminded me of a time when things were less complicated. We arranged to meet up later that week at a small café we used to frequent. I had my reservations—what if he didn't understand what I was going through? But deep down, I knew I needed this. I needed to reconnect with someone who knew the real me, not the version of myself I showed to the world.

When I walked into the café, I felt a mix of emotions—nostalgia, anxiety, and a sliver of hope. Rohan was already there, sitting at our old spot by the window. He looked the same as he always had, with an easygoing smile and a calm demeanor that put me at ease. We exchanged pleasantries, talked about what we'd been up to, but there was an unspoken understanding that we would eventually get to the real reason I had reached out.

After a few minutes, Rohan leaned back in his chair and looked at me thoughtfully. "So, what's really going on, Aryan? You don't seem like yourself."

His words hit me harder than I expected. For a moment, I didn't know how to respond. But then, the floodgates opened. I told him everything—the pressure, the stress, the mistakes, the growing sense of emptiness that had been gnawing at me for months. As I spoke, I could see Rohan listening intently, not judging, just absorbing everything I was saying. When I finally stopped, I felt a weight lift off my shoulders. I had never been this honest with anyone in a long time, not even with myself.

Rohan didn't say anything right away. He took a sip of his coffee, seemingly lost in thought. When he finally spoke, his words were direct but filled with concern. "Aryan, I've seen what you've been doing online, and yeah, it's impressive. But it's not real. It's like you're living in this bubble, and everything outside of it doesn't exist. You've got all these people following you, but how many of them actually know you? I mean, the real you?"

His words stung, but they were exactly what I needed to hear. He wasn't saying anything I hadn't already thought myself, but hearing it from someone else—someone who knew me before all of this—made it all the more real.

"You were always so grounded," Rohan continued. "Back in the day, you didn't care about what other people thought. You were just... you. Now it seems like you're constantly trying to live up to this impossible standard, and for what? Likes? Followers? Is it really worth it?"

I didn't have an answer. How could I? Everything I had built was based on those very things—likes, followers, validation from strangers on the internet. But sitting there with Rohan, I began to see just how hollow it all was. It wasn't worth the anxiety, the sleepless nights, the constant fear of failure. For the first time, I started to see the cracks in my digital facade not as failures, but as opportunities. Opportunities to change, to step back, to rediscover the person I used to be.

"Maybe you're right," I finally admitted, the words feeling foreign yet freeing. "But where do I even start? This is all I've known for so long."

Rohan smiled, a small, reassuring smile that reminded me of simpler times. "You start by being honest with yourself. Figure out what really matters to you, and not just what you think matters to everyone else. Maybe it's time to take a break, step away from the spotlight for a bit, and find out what you want your life to look like—beyond the screen."

His words were a revelation. For so long, I had been so focused on maintaining my online image that I had lost sight of everything else. The idea of stepping away from it all was terrifying, but it was also the first time I had felt a glimmer of hope in what seemed like forever. Maybe, just maybe, there was a way out of this mess—a way to find balance, to reconnect with who I was before the fame, and to build a life that felt genuine and fulfilling.

As we left the café, I felt a sense of clarity that had been missing for so long. The path ahead was uncertain, and I knew it wouldn't be easy, but for the first time, I felt like I had a choice. I could continue down the road I was on, or I could take a step back and start making changes—small at first, but changes nonetheless.

Rohan's words stayed with me as I walked home, and for the first time in a long while, I felt like I could breathe. The first glimpse of change had appeared on the horizon, and though I didn't know where it would lead, I knew one thing for sure—I was ready to find out.

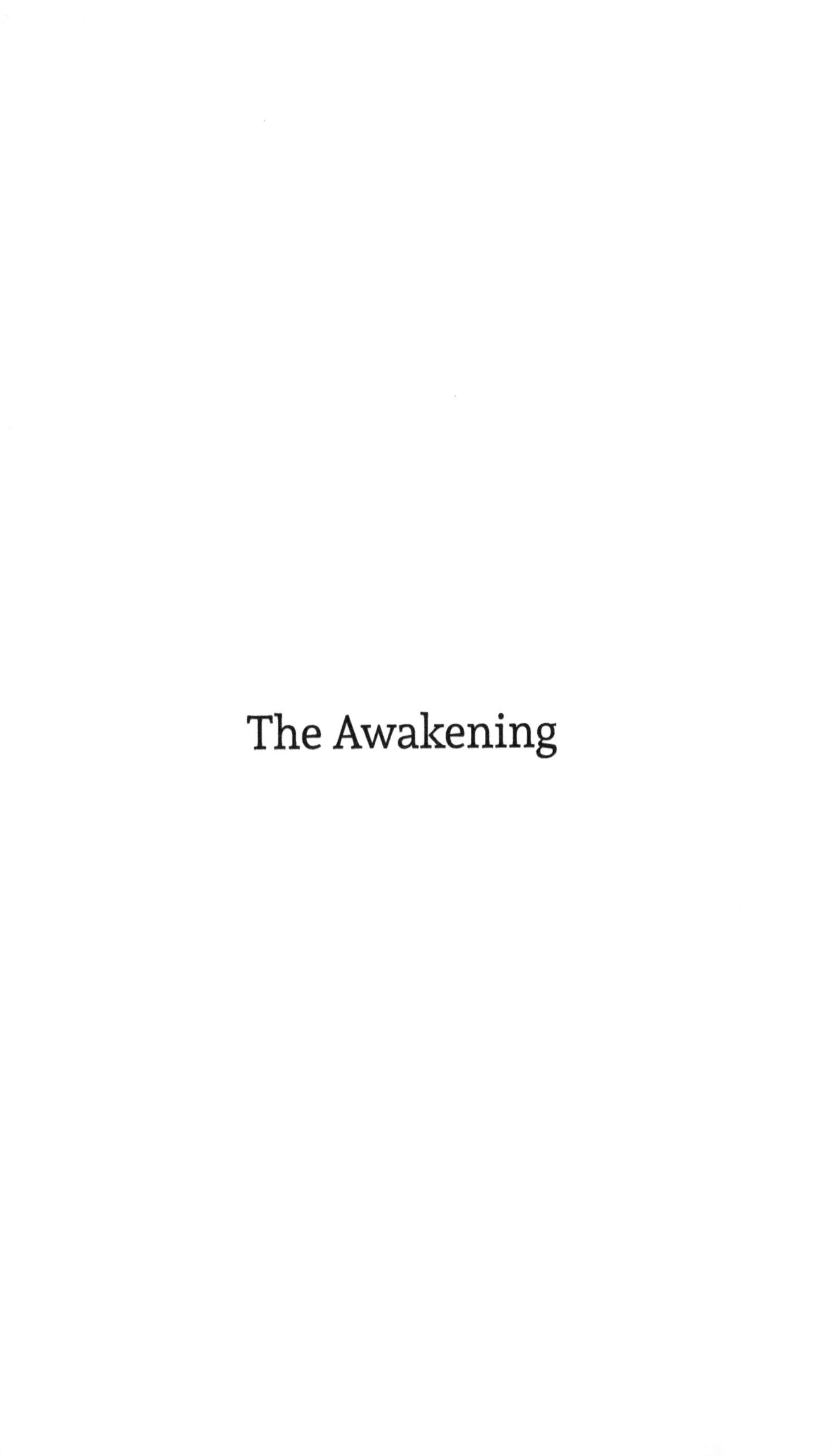

The Awakening

11

Reflecting on the Past

The days following my conversation with Rohan were filled with a strange, restless energy. It was as if a dam had broken inside me, releasing a flood of emotions and memories I had kept buried for years. I couldn't stop thinking about what he had said, his words echoing in my mind like a persistent melody that refused to fade.

"You were just... you." The simplicity of that statement was what struck me the most. When had I stopped being just me? When had I become this person who cared more about likes and followers than the things that once brought me genuine happiness? I didn't have the answers, but I knew I needed to find them.

I started to actively reflect on my life before social media took over. It wasn't easy—those memories felt distant, like scenes from an old movie that I could barely remember. But slowly, they began to surface, and with them came a bittersweet sense of nostalgia.

I remembered the early mornings spent jogging in the park, feeling the cool breeze against my skin and the satisfaction of pushing my body to its limits. Back then, exercise wasn't something I did for the sake of appearances or to fit a certain image; it was something I did because it made me feel alive, connected to the world around me.

I thought about the afternoons spent reading, losing myself in the pages of a good book. There was a time when I could spend hours in a quiet corner of a library or a café, completely engrossed in a story that transported me to another world. Reading had once been my escape, my way of exploring new ideas and perspectives, but in recent years, I had barely picked up a book. The time I used to spend reading had been replaced by endless scrolling, chasing the latest trends, and obsessing over engagement metrics.

Then there were the evenings with my family, the simple joy of being in their company, sharing stories, and laughing together. I couldn't remember the last time I had sat down with them without my phone in hand, fully present in the moment. The realization hit me hard—how much had I missed out on in my pursuit of an online persona that was only a fraction of who I really was?

As these memories flooded back, I felt a deep sense of loss. I had sacrificed so much for the sake of a digital world that, in the end, felt empty and unfulfilling. The things that had once brought me joy—exercise, reading, time with family—had all been pushed aside, replaced by the constant need to maintain a facade of perfection. It was a bitter pill to swallow, but one that I knew I needed to confront if I was ever going to find a way forward.

The more I reflected, the more I realized just how far I had strayed from the person I used to be. I had become so consumed by the pursuit of success in the online world that I had lost sight of what truly mattered. My life had become a series of carefully curated moments, designed to impress strangers on the internet, while the things that once gave my life meaning had slipped through my fingers like sand.

But along with the sadness came a sense of clarity. I didn't have to continue down this path. I had the power to change, to reconnect with the things that made me feel whole. It wouldn't be easy, and I knew I couldn't undo the past, but I could start making different choices—choices that would lead me back to a life that felt authentic and fulfilling.

One evening, I found myself standing in front of my bookshelf, a collection of books that had been gathering dust for far too long. I reached out and pulled down a novel I had once loved, its pages yellowed with age. As I opened it, the familiar scent of old paper filled the air, bringing back memories of countless hours spent lost in stories that had shaped my understanding of the world.

I sat down and began to read, letting the words wash over me. For the first time in what felt like forever, I was fully present in the moment, not thinking about the next post or the next trend. It was just me and the story, and in that moment, I felt a connection to something deeper, something real.

As I read, I couldn't help but smile. The past wasn't something to dwell on with regret; it was a reminder of what I was capable of, what I could bring back into my life. Reflecting on who I used to be wasn't just about mourning what I had lost—it was about finding a way to reclaim it.

That night, as I lay in bed, I made a promise to myself. I would continue to reflect, to remember the things that once brought me joy, and to find ways to reintroduce them into my life. It was time to start living for myself again, not for the approval of others. It was time to rediscover the person I had been before the world of social media took over.

And so, as sleep finally claimed me, I felt a sense of peace that had eluded me for so long. The journey ahead was uncertain, but I was ready to take the next step, to continue the process of awakening to a life that felt true to who I really was.

12
The Search for Meaning

Determined to find meaning beyond the digital world, I decided it was time to explore new interests and hobbies. I needed to rediscover what it meant to live a life that wasn't dictated by likes and followers. It wasn't going to be easy, but the desire for something more meaningful kept pushing me forward.

I started with something familiar—photography. There was a time when I loved taking photos purely for the joy of capturing moments, not for the attention they would garner online. I dug out my old camera, a simple device compared to the high-end equipment I now used for work, and ventured out to find inspiration in the world beyond my screen.

As I walked around my neighborhood, I noticed things I hadn't paid attention to in years—the rustling of leaves, the soft chirping of birds, the way sunlight filtered through the trees. Everything felt new, vibrant, like I was seeing it all for the first time. I found myself smiling, truly enjoying the simplicity of just being in the moment.

With each photo I took, I focused on how it made me feel, not how it would look online. The process was therapeutic, reminding me of who I used to be before my online persona took over. It wasn't about creating content; it was about capturing life as it happened, raw and unfiltered.

But breaking away from old habits wasn't easy. The urge to share my work online, to seek validation from my followers, was strong. I had to constantly remind myself that this was for me, not for them. The first few days were tough; I'd reach for my phone out of habit, only to stop myself and focus on what was in front of me. Gradually, the need to check my social media began to fade, replaced by a growing appreciation for the present moment.

I also started exploring other hobbies I had long forgotten. Cooking, for instance, became a new passion. I tried out recipes I had never attempted before, and the act of preparing a meal from scratch, of tasting and adjusting flavors, brought me a sense of accomplishment that was different from the instant gratification of likes and comments. It felt real, tangible, and satisfying in a way that social media had never been.

I even picked up a book—a real, physical book, not an e-book or an audiobook. It had been years since I'd read anything for pleasure, and it felt almost foreign to me. But as I got lost in the story, I realized how much I had missed the simple joy of reading. The words on the page transported me to another world, one where the pressures of maintaining an online image didn't exist.

These small but significant changes helped me start rediscovering who I was outside of the digital realm. The process was slow, sometimes frustrating, but it was also deeply rewarding. I began to remember the person I used to be, someone who found joy in the little things, who lived life for the experiences, not for the validation of others.

The search for meaning became my new obsession, replacing the hollow pursuit of online fame. I knew I wasn't there yet, that I still had a long way to go, but the journey itself was starting to feel like the reward. Each day brought a new discovery, a new piece of the puzzle that was my true self. And with each step forward, I felt a little more like the person I had lost along the way.

13

A Mysterious Message

The familiar ping of a notification pulled me out of my thoughts. I had been avoiding my phone, trying to immerse myself in my newfound hobbies, but the curiosity got the better of me. When I unlocked the screen, there it was—another message from the mysterious person.

This time, the message was different. It wasn't just a simple question like before; it was more personal, more direct. "I remember the old you, the one who was full of life and passion. Where did he go?"

The words hit me like a punch to the gut. Whoever this person was, they seemed to know me—really know me. Not the version of me that I projected online, but the real me, the one I had almost forgotten existed. My heart raced as I read the message over and over, trying to make sense of it.

Who could it be? An old friend? A former classmate? Someone who knew me before the fame, before the carefully curated life I had built online? The possibilities swirled in my mind, each one more puzzling than the last. I couldn't shake the feeling that this person knew something about me that even I had forgotten.

The message deepened my curiosity and stirred a longing for the person I used to be. The more I thought about it, the more I realized how much I missed that version of myself—the one who was passionate about life, who wasn't obsessed with likes and followers, who found joy in the simple things.

But who was this person, and how did they know me so well? I felt a strange mix of excitement and unease. On one hand, I wanted to find out who they were, to confront them and ask how they knew so much about me. On the other hand, I was afraid of what I might discover. What if they saw through the facade I had built, saw the cracks in my carefully constructed image? What if they knew the truth—that I wasn't as happy or as successful as I appeared to be?

I knew I couldn't ignore the message, though. There was something about it that compelled me to dig deeper, to uncover the identity of this mysterious person. But how? The message was sent from an anonymous account, no profile picture, no real name, just a string of random numbers and letters. It was as if this person didn't want to be found, yet they were reaching out to me in a way that felt almost intimate.

I decided to reply, hoping to draw them out, to get some clue as to who they were. My fingers hovered over the keyboard as I thought about what to say. I didn't want to sound too desperate or too casual, so I settled on something simple.

"Who are you?"

I stared at the screen for a few seconds before hitting send. As the message went through, I felt a knot of anxiety tighten in my stomach. Would they respond? Would they reveal themselves? Or would this be the last I heard from them?

The minutes ticked by slowly as I waited for a reply. I tried to distract myself by picking up my camera and snapping a few photos, but my mind kept drifting back to the mysterious message. Who could it be? And what did they want from me?

Just as I was about to give up and put my phone away, it buzzed again. Another message. My heart pounded as I opened it.

"You already know who I am."

The words sent a chill down my spine. What did they mean? Was this someone I knew well, someone from my past? Or was it just another mind game, meant to keep me guessing?

The mystery only deepened my resolve to find out who was behind these messages. I had to know. Not just for the sake of curiosity, but because this person seemed to hold the key to unlocking a part of myself I had long buried.

I had to figure out who they were—and, more importantly, who I really was beneath the layers of fame and influence I had wrapped around myself.

14

Attempts at Reconnection

I knew it was time to reconnect with my old friends—the ones who had known me before my life revolved around filters, hashtags, and sponsored posts. These were the people who had seen me at my worst and my best, back when life was simpler and our biggest worries were mundane, like where to hang out on a Friday night or which movie to catch. But now, years later, I couldn't shake the feeling that those connections had frayed, slipping away as I climbed higher into the world of influence.

With a mix of anticipation and dread, I decided to start small. I scrolled through my contacts, pausing at names that once meant so much to me but had become little more than symbols on a screen. I settled on calling Sam, my best friend from college. Back then, we had been inseparable, bonded by our shared love of music, late-night gaming sessions, and dreams that felt boundless. But as I hesitated over the call button, I realized I hadn't spoken to him in nearly three years. What would I even say?

The phone rang several times, and I found myself hoping it would go to voicemail. When Sam finally picked up, his voice was warm but slightly guarded. "Aryan? Wow, it's been a while," he said, and I could almost hear the smile in his voice.

"Yeah, it has," I replied, my own voice sounding foreign to me. "I thought it was time to catch up."

The conversation that followed was stilted, punctuated by awkward pauses. We talked about the basics—work, life, the weather—but it was clear that we were both struggling to find common ground. The easy camaraderie we once shared was missing. Instead of the lively debates and laughter that used to define our talks, there was a careful politeness, as if we were both trying to avoid saying the wrong thing.

I decided to push through the discomfort. "Hey, why don't we meet up in person? It's been too long, and I'd love to catch up properly."

Sam agreed, though I could sense his hesitation. We set a date for the following weekend, at a coffee shop we used to frequent. As I hung up, I felt a mix of relief and anxiety. The first step was done, but what would happen when we were face to face?

The day of our meeting, I arrived early, my nerves jangling. The coffee shop was just as I remembered—dimly lit, with mismatched chairs and the comforting aroma of freshly brewed coffee. But as I sat there waiting, I realized how much I had changed. Back then, I would have been engrossed in a conversation, laughing with Sam about something trivial. Now, I was more conscious of my appearance, my phone, and the number of likes my latest post was getting.

When Sam walked in, I almost didn't recognize him. He had changed too—his hair was shorter, his clothes more professional, and there was a subtle weariness in his eyes. We exchanged an awkward hug, and as we sat down, I noticed the distance between us, both physical and emotional.

We started with small talk, catching up on the years we had missed. Sam told me about his job, his new apartment, and a recent hiking trip he had taken with his girlfriend. I listened, trying to engage, but I felt like I was playing a role rather than being present. The conversation felt forced, and I could tell Sam was aware of it too.

After a while, Sam paused, looking at me intently. "You know, Aryan, I've been following you on social media. It's amazing what you've accomplished."

I smiled, but it didn't reach my eyes. "Thanks, man. It's been a wild ride."

He nodded, but there was a hint of something in his expression—concern, maybe even sadness. "But is it really you? The Aryan I knew was different. More... real, I guess."

His words hit me harder than I expected. "I'm still me," I said, though I wasn't entirely sure if I believed it.

"Are you?" Sam's tone was gentle, but his words cut deep. "I remember when we used to spend hours talking about music, philosophy, and all the things that made life worth living. Now, it seems like your life is more about... the image."

I looked down at my coffee, swirling it absentmindedly. "It's complicated," I finally said. "This world I'm in—it's not easy to separate the image from the person."

Sam sighed, leaning back in his chair. "I get that. But I miss the old Aryan, the one who didn't care about what people thought, who was just... there, in the moment."

His words hung in the air, and for the first time in a long while, I felt something shift inside me. The conversation that followed was more honest than anything I'd had in years. We talked about the pressures I faced, the loneliness that came with fame, and the fear of losing everything if I let my guard down.

By the time we finished, the awkwardness had faded, replaced by a tentative understanding. As we parted ways, Sam clapped me on the shoulder. "It was good to see you, Aryan. Don't be a stranger."

"I won't," I promised, and this time, I meant it.

But the encounter left me shaken. Reconnecting with Sam had been more difficult than I anticipated, and it forced me to confront the reality of how much I had changed. I had expected a warm, easy reunion, but instead, I was faced with the uncomfortable truth that the person I had become wasn't someone I entirely recognized—or liked.

Over the next few weeks, I reached out to other friends from my past, hoping to rekindle those old connections. But each encounter was met with similar challenges. The laughter didn't come as easily, the conversations felt strained, and the shared memories that once bonded us seemed distant and irrelevant.

One night, I met up with a group of friends from high school. We gathered at a familiar hangout spot, a dingy bar that had been our go-to back in the day. As we sat around a table, drinking and reminiscing, I couldn't shake the feeling that I didn't belong anymore. They talked about their jobs, their families, and the little moments that made up their lives, while I struggled to contribute anything meaningful. My stories felt shallow, disconnected from the realities they were describing.

At one point, one of my friends, Raj, turned to me and asked, "So, Aryan, what's it like being famous? You must be living the dream."

I forced a smile, knowing they wouldn't understand the full weight of my answer. "It's... different. Not always what it seems."

"Come on," another friend chimed in, laughing. "You've got everything—money, followers, a lifestyle most people would kill for. What's not to love?"

I wanted to tell them the truth—that the life they envied was often empty, that the pressure to maintain a perfect image was suffocating, and that I missed the days when I could just be myself without worrying about how it would be perceived. But instead, I just nodded along, letting them believe what they wanted to believe.

As the night wore on, I found myself retreating into my thoughts, feeling more isolated than ever. The people around me had moved on with their lives, while I had been stuck in a cycle of seeking validation from strangers online. The realization was painful, but it was also necessary. I had been so focused on maintaining an image that I had lost sight of what truly mattered—genuine connections, real conversations, and the simple joys of being present in the moment.

When the night finally ended, I walked home alone, the cool breeze doing little to calm the storm of emotions inside me. Reconnecting with my old friends had been anything but simple. It was a harsh reminder that time changes everything, and that the life I had built was not as fulfilling as I had convinced myself it was.

But as difficult as it was, these attempts at reconnection were also a turning point. They forced me to confront the reality of my situation, to acknowledge the emptiness that had been growing inside me for years. And while I didn't have all the answers yet, I knew one thing for sure: I couldn't keep living the way I had been. Something had to change, and it had to start with me.

15

The First Failure

After my meeting with Sam, the thought of reconnecting with another old friend felt both daunting and necessary. Sam had been a close friend, but the distance that time had put between us made me realize how much I had changed. Still, I needed to try again. If I could just find someone who could remind me of who I used to be, maybe I could rediscover that part of myself.

I decided to reach out to Ravi, someone who had been my best friend during our college days. Ravi was different from Sam; he was the kind of person who could make anyone feel at ease. We hadn't spoken in years, but I remembered the countless nights we spent talking about our dreams, the pranks we played, and the way he always encouraged me to chase my passions.

I sent Ravi a message, and to my surprise, he responded quickly. He seemed enthusiastic about catching up, which gave me a glimmer of hope. We arranged to meet at a quiet park where we used to hang out, a place that held memories of carefree days and endless conversations.

As I walked to the park, I couldn't help but feel nervous. The last time I had tried to reconnect with an old friend, it hadn't gone well. But I told myself that this time would be different. Ravi had always been someone who understood me, someone who could see beyond the surface.

When I arrived, Ravi was already there, sitting on a bench under a large oak tree. He waved as I approached, and I could see the familiar twinkle in his eyes. For a moment, I felt like I was stepping back in time.

"Hey, Aryan!" Ravi greeted me with a warm smile. "It's been too long."

"Yeah, it really has," I replied, returning his smile as we shook hands.

We sat down and started talking, reminiscing about the old days. Ravi was just as I remembered—easygoing, with a quick wit and a knack for making me laugh. For a while, it felt like nothing had changed. We talked about our college days, the professors we loved and hated, and the adventures we had together. It was comforting, like slipping into a familiar routine.

But as the conversation shifted to the present, the gap between our lives became apparent. Ravi talked about his career, his family, and the community work he was involved in. He seemed genuinely fulfilled, content with the life he had built. When it was my turn to talk, I hesitated. I knew how my life would sound to him—shallow, superficial, and driven by a relentless pursuit of validation.

I tried to explain what I did, how I had become a social media influencer, but the words felt empty as they left my mouth. Ravi listened politely, but I could see the confusion in his eyes. He didn't understand the world I was living in, and I couldn't blame him. It was a world that was all about appearances, where relationships were transactional, and where the line between reality and fiction was constantly blurred.

As I spoke, I realized how disconnected I had become from the things that once mattered to me. Ravi asked me about my hobbies, the things I did for fun, and I found myself struggling to answer. My life had become so consumed by my online persona that there was little room for anything else.

The conversation grew increasingly strained. The more I talked, the more I felt the weight of the distance between us. Ravi tried to bridge the gap, asking questions, trying to find common ground, but it was clear that we were living in different worlds. The connection we once shared was slipping away, and no matter how hard I tried, I couldn't bring it back.

Finally, after what felt like an eternity, Ravi looked at me with a sad smile and said, "It's good to see you, Aryan. But I have to be honest—I miss the old you. The guy who was passionate about life, who didn't care about what others thought."

His words hit me like a punch to the gut. I nodded, unable to find the right words to respond. I wanted to tell him that I missed that guy too, that I was trying to find him again, but the words stuck in my throat.

We ended the conversation on a polite note, promising to stay in touch, but we both knew that things would never be the same. As I walked away from the park, I felt a deep sense of failure. I had hoped that reconnecting with Ravi would help me reclaim a part of myself, but instead, it only highlighted how far I had strayed from the person I used to be.

Doubt began to creep in, gnawing at me as I replayed the conversation in my mind. What if I couldn't go back? What if the person I used to be was gone forever? The thought was terrifying. I had built my life around my online persona, but now that it was starting to crumble, I wasn't sure if there was anything left underneath.

For the first time, I wondered if I had lost myself for good.

16
Family Dynamics

I sat on the edge of my bed, staring at the framed photographs on the wall. They showed me at different stages of my life—my childhood, early adolescence, and moments with my family. Each photo felt like a snapshot of a time when things were simpler, when my biggest concerns were school projects and weekend plans rather than social media metrics and public perception.

It had been a long time since I felt truly connected with my family. The warmth and familiarity that used to define our interactions had been replaced by a cold formality. My rise to fame had changed so much, not just for me but for everyone around me. I knew I needed to fix things before it was too late.

My parents had been my biggest supporters, but their support seemed to have turned into silent disappointment. My father, who had always been a pillar of strength, now seemed distant. I could see the strain in his eyes, a reflection of the unspoken words between us. My mother, the emotional anchor of our family, had taken to long walks alone, and her gaze often lingered on old photo albums with a sorrowful look. My younger siblings, Mia and Arjun, who had once been so close to me, had retreated into their own worlds. Our conversations had become strained, often ending in awkward silence or superficial exchanges.

The turning point came one evening when I decided it was time to address the distance that had grown between us. I gathered everyone in the living room, the heart of our home that had once been filled with laughter and conversation. The smell of my mother's cooking still lingered in the air, a comforting reminder of the way things used to be.

"Can we talk?" I asked, my voice unsteady. I wasn't sure how this would go, but I knew it was necessary.

My father nodded, his expression unreadable. My mother's eyes softened, though they were still tinged with sadness. Mia and Arjun exchanged glances, their faces mirroring a mix of curiosity and apprehension.

I took a deep breath, struggling to find the right words. "I know things haven't been the same. I've been so wrapped up in my career, in maintaining my image, that I didn't realize how much I was pushing you all away. I'm sorry for not being there when it mattered."

My father shifted, finally breaking his silence. "Aryan, we're proud of what you've achieved, but it feels like we've lost you. You're always so busy, always chasing the next thing. We miss the real you, not the person you present online."

My mother reached out and gently touched my hand. "We've always been here for you, but it feels like you've built a wall between us. We want to be part of your life, but we need to feel like we matter."

Mia, who usually kept to herself, finally spoke. "You used to be so present in our lives. We had so much fun together. Now, it feels like we're just watching from the sidelines."

I felt a lump in my throat as I listened to their words. The realization of how much I had neglected them in my pursuit of success hit me hard. I had been so focused on building a public image that I had lost sight of the people who mattered most.

"I've been selfish," I admitted, my voice cracking. "I let my career come between us, and I see now how much that has hurt all of you. I want to change that. I want to be the brother, son, and friend you deserve."

My father's stern expression softened, and my mother squeezed my hand reassuringly. "It's not too late, Aryan. We can work through this together. It will take time, but we're willing to try if you are."

We spent the rest of the evening talking, sharing our feelings and concerns. We reminisced about happy memories and discussed our current lives and future hopes. For the first time in a long while, I felt a genuine connection with my family. It was a feeling I realized I wanted to hold onto.

As I walked back to my room that night, I felt a renewed sense of hope. Repairing these relationships wouldn't be easy, but I was ready to put in the effort. I knew it would take time, patience, and dedication, but I was determined to find a balance and rediscover the happiness that had been missing for so long.

17

A Turning Point

The days following my heart-to-heart with my family were filled with a mix of reflection and determination. I felt a renewed sense of purpose, but I knew I needed something more—a deeper conversation that would truly steer me back on course. That's when I decided to talk to Mia.

Mia had always been the quiet one, the one who observed more than she spoke. But I knew there was wisdom in her silence, and I hoped she could offer me some insight. I asked her to join me for coffee at our favorite café, a place we used to visit together before my life got swallowed by fame.

The café was bustling with the usual afternoon crowd, but the familiar scent of coffee and baked goods brought a sense of comfort. We found a quiet corner, away from the noise, and settled into our seats. Mia looked at me with a mixture of curiosity and apprehension, her hands wrapped around her coffee cup.

"I'm glad we could do this," I said, trying to sound casual but feeling a bit nervous. "I've been thinking a lot lately, and I really need to talk to you."

Mia nodded, her eyes attentive. "What's on your mind, Aryan?"

I took a deep breath, struggling to find the right words. "I've been feeling so disconnected lately, from everything and everyone. It's like I've been living in a bubble, chasing after something that doesn't really matter. I've been so focused on my career and public image that I've lost sight of what's important. I want to change that, but I'm not sure how."

Mia's gaze softened, and she took a sip of her coffee before responding. "I've seen how hard you've worked and how much you've accomplished, but I've also seen how it's changed you. It's like you're living for an audience rather than for yourself and the people who care about you."

I nodded, feeling a lump form in my throat. "I know. It's been hard to admit, but I realize now that I've been chasing validation instead of genuine connections. I miss the way things used to be, the way we used to be."

Mia's expression grew serious as she leaned in slightly. "Do you remember what Dad always used to say? About staying true to yourself and not letting external pressures define who you are?"

I nodded, a faint smile crossing my face. "Of course. He always said that our values are what keep us grounded."

Mia continued, her voice steady but gentle. "I think it's time you went back to those values. You've always been someone who valued real connections over superficial ones. Maybe it's time to realign yourself with that part of who you are. It's okay to seek success, but don't lose yourself in the process."

Her words struck a chord deep within me. I realized that despite the fame and the accolades, I had strayed from the person I used to be—the person who valued family, friendship, and authenticity above all else.

"You're right," I said, my voice breaking slightly. "I've been so caught up in this whirlwind of success that I forgot what really matters. I want to find a way back to who I was, to what I believe in."

Mia reached across the table and took my hand. "It's not going to be easy, Aryan. There will be challenges, and you'll have to make choices that might not always be popular. But you're stronger than you think. Just remember to stay true to yourself, and the rest will follow."

I squeezed her hand, feeling a surge of gratitude. "Thank you, Mia. I needed to hear that. It's hard to see things clearly when you're so deep in the middle of it all. Your perspective really helped."

As we finished our coffee and talked more about our plans and hopes for the future, I felt a renewed sense of clarity. Mia's words had given me a new perspective, a turning point in my journey. I understood now that real success wasn't just about public recognition but about maintaining genuine relationships and staying true to my values.

Leaving the café, I felt a sense of resolve. I knew the road ahead would be challenging, but I was ready to face it with a renewed commitment to myself and to those who mattered most. It was time to move forward, to rebuild the connections that had been strained, and to rediscover the happiness that came from living a life aligned with my true values.

18

Exploring Offline Interests

The days following my conversation with Mia felt like a slow but necessary unraveling of my tightly wound world. I had resolved to reconnect with my core values, and part of that journey meant revisiting the parts of myself I had left behind. One evening, as I sifted through old boxes in the attic, I stumbled upon a dusty, forgotten camera—my old photography gear.

It was a Nikon D90, a relic from a time when I was passionate about capturing moments through a lens. I remembered the joy I used to find in photography, how each click of the shutter felt like a discovery, a way to see the world through a different perspective. I hadn't touched the camera in years, having set it aside in favor of the ever-demanding world of social media and public appearances.

With a mixture of nostalgia and anticipation, I decided to dust off the old camera and take it for a spin. I found myself wandering through the city, feeling a sense of liberation with each step. The streets that had once seemed mundane now held a new potential for discovery. My mind was free from the constant buzz of notifications and the pressure of maintaining an online image.

As I walked through a nearby park, I began to notice the small, beautiful details I had once taken for granted—the golden light filtering through the leaves, the intricate patterns on the petals of flowers, the way children's laughter echoed through the air. I started taking photos, not for any particular purpose but simply for the joy of capturing what I saw.

The act of photography brought a sense of peace I hadn't felt in years. Each image was a reminder of the simple pleasures I had overlooked. The sound of the shutter clicking, the focus on finding the right angle, and the satisfaction of viewing the final shot on the screen—it all felt grounding and fulfilling.

After a few hours of exploring and photographing, I found a quiet spot by a lake and sat down to review my shots. I was struck by the realization that I had missed this. The feeling of being fully immersed in an activity that had nothing to do with fame or social media was refreshing. It was a return to a simpler, more authentic version of myself.

Photography wasn't the only interest I had set aside. As I delved into this old hobby, I began to think about other passions I had neglected. Music, for example. I had once been an avid guitar player, spending hours strumming and composing songs. It was another part of my life that had been overshadowed by the demands of my career.

The following weekend, I dug out my old guitar from the closet. It had gathered dust, but as I strummed the first few chords, I felt a wave of nostalgia. The music that had once been a form of self-expression and escape now seemed like a bridge back to a more genuine version of myself. I spent hours playing and singing, reconnecting with the melodies that had once filled my life with joy.

Revisiting these interests wasn't just about indulging in pastimes; it was about rediscovering parts of myself that had been overshadowed by my public persona. Each moment spent with my camera or guitar felt like a small but significant step towards reclaiming my identity and finding balance.

As I continued to explore these offline interests, I noticed a shift in my overall well-being. There was a sense of fulfillment and contentment that had been missing for too long. The pressure of maintaining a certain image or meeting the expectations of others began to wane, replaced by a renewed focus on what genuinely made me happy.

I also started setting aside time for these activities regularly, integrating them back into my life as a way to maintain that sense of peace and connection. It wasn't always easy to balance these interests with my public commitments, but I was determined to make it work. Each small step, each moment of joy, was a reaffirmation of my commitment to rediscovering and nurturing the person I had once been.

In these moments of solitude and creativity, I found that I was slowly but surely finding my way back to myself. The journey was far from over, but I felt hopeful and encouraged. Revisiting these offline interests was more than just a hobby—it was a path to healing and rediscovery, a way to reconnect with what truly mattered and to start building a more balanced and fulfilling life.

19
The Digital Backlash

It was early morning when I first noticed the shift. As I scrolled through my social media feed, I saw the numbers—follower counts dropping, engagement levels plummeting. My once vibrant, buzzing profile now seemed eerily quiet. The comments that had once been filled with praise and adoration were now tinged with criticism and disappointment.

"Where have you been? You used to post so much!" one comment read.

"Is this the end of your career? You don't seem to care about us anymore," another said.

I took a deep breath and closed my laptop. The pang of anxiety was immediate, but it was quickly followed by an unexpected sense of calm. This was the backlash I had anticipated, and despite the initial sting, there was a profound sense of relief in the realization that I was finally letting go of my dependence on constant validation.

For years, my life had been a relentless cycle of content creation, public appearances, and managing my online image. Every like, share, and comment had become a measure of my worth. My worth, however, had been entangled with the numbers and the feedback loop of social media. Now that I was stepping back from this demanding role, the consequences were becoming clear.

I spent the rest of the day away from my devices, focusing on the offline activities that had recently become a source of joy and fulfillment. I walked through the park with my camera, capturing images of the world around me, savoring the peaceful moments. I picked up my guitar and lost myself in playing melodies that spoke to my soul, rather than to an audience.

In these moments, the digital backlash seemed to fade into the background. I felt a sense of liberation from the constant need for approval. The joy I experienced from reconnecting with my hobbies was far more satisfying than any amount of online praise could ever be.

Later that week, I met up with a close friend, Raj, who had been a steadfast supporter throughout my career. He noticed the shift in my demeanor and was quick to ask about it.

"You seem different lately," Raj remarked as we sat down for coffee. "What's going on?"

I hesitated before speaking, unsure of how to articulate the transformation I was undergoing. "I've been stepping back from social media. I needed a break, and I'm starting to realize how much I relied on it for validation. The backlash I'm getting now is intense, but it's also freeing. It's like I'm finally starting to let go of the need to constantly seek approval."

Raj's expression softened with understanding. "That sounds like a tough but important step. It's easy to get caught up in the whirlwind of online fame and lose sight of what really matters. I'm glad you're finding peace in other areas of your life."

Our conversation continued, and Raj offered insights and encouragement that helped me solidify my resolve. The backlash wasn't just a setback; it was a turning point. It forced me to confront the emptiness that had been masked by the façade of social media success.

As the weeks passed, I noticed that while the criticism continued, it no longer had the same power over me. The negative comments and dropping follower counts were reminders of my shift in priorities. I was no longer the person who sought constant validation from a screen. Instead, I was someone rediscovering what it meant to find genuine fulfillment and happiness.

The digital world had become less of a focus, and my offline life was blossoming. I was reconnecting with friends, spending quality time with my family, and immersing myself in my passions. The fear of losing my online presence was overshadowed by the joy of rediscovering myself.

In the end, the digital backlash became a catalyst for my personal growth. It pushed me to confront my insecurities and to redefine my sense of worth. I learned that true contentment comes from within, not from the fleeting approval of an online audience. As I moved forward, I embraced the freedom that came with letting go of the need for constant validation and welcomed the genuine connections and experiences that awaited me in the real world.

20
A New Circle

As the weeks turned into months, the changes in my life became more pronounced. I was spending less time online and more time engaging with the world around me. The photography excursions that had started as solitary outings soon led me to places where other photographers gathered. I began to meet people who shared my passion for capturing the world through a lens, and gradually, a new circle of friends started to form around me.

It began with a chance encounter at a local photography workshop. I had signed up on a whim, eager to improve my skills and connect with others who loved the craft. The workshop was held in a cozy studio space, its walls lined with striking black-and-white prints. The instructor, an experienced photographer named Neha, had a warm, approachable demeanor that immediately put everyone at ease.

As we introduced ourselves, I realized I wasn't the only one seeking something deeper than the superficial connections I had grown accustomed to. The other participants were a diverse group—students, professionals, hobbyists—all drawn together by a shared love of photography. There was a genuine enthusiasm in the room, a sense of camaraderie that felt refreshingly different from the competitive atmosphere of social media.

During a break, I struck up a conversation with a guy named Rohan. He was a freelance photographer with a knack for street photography. We talked about our favorite techniques, our inspirations, and soon enough, our conversation shifted to the broader topic of life outside the digital world.

"I used to be really into social media," Rohan admitted, sipping his coffee. "But it started feeling so empty, you know? I realized I was spending more time curating my life online than actually living it."

His words resonated with me. "That's exactly where I've been. I'm trying to reconnect with what really matters, and photography has been a big part of that."

Rohan nodded, a knowing smile on his face. "It's good to find people who get it. I've found that real-life connections, the ones you make over shared passions, are so much more meaningful. You should join our photography meet-ups. We're a small group, but it's a great way to keep the inspiration flowing and meet like-minded people."

I took him up on his offer, and over the next few weeks, I found myself becoming a regular at these gatherings. The group met every other Saturday, choosing different locations around the city to explore and photograph. We'd spend hours wandering through markets, parks, and hidden alleys, capturing the essence of everyday life. The conversations were as enriching as the photography itself—discussions about technique flowed naturally into deeper talks about life, art, and our shared desire for authenticity.

It wasn't just about photography, either. Through this new circle, I began to meet people who introduced me to other offline activities—hiking, cooking classes, even the occasional open mic night where I found the courage to play my guitar in front of a small, supportive audience. These experiences were far removed from the digital world I had once been so consumed by, but they brought me a level of satisfaction I hadn't felt in years.

One evening, after a particularly rewarding photo walk, our group gathered at a local café to review our shots and share stories. As I looked around the table, I felt an overwhelming sense of belonging. These people didn't care about how many followers I had or what my latest post was about. They valued me for who I was, not the persona I had created online.

Neha, the instructor from the workshop who had become a mentor of sorts, smiled at me from across the table. "You've really found your groove, Aryan. It's great to see how passionate you are about this. And it's even better to see how you've connected with everyone here."

I nodded, feeling a warmth in my chest that was unfamiliar but welcome. "I didn't realize how much I needed this—a community that values real connections, not just surface-level interactions. It's been a long time since I've felt this comfortable just being myself."

Rohan raised his glass in a toast. "To new friends and new beginnings."

We all joined in, clinking our glasses together. It was a simple moment, but it held so much meaning. For the first time in a long time, I felt like I was part of something real. I was surrounded by people who understood me, who valued the same things I did, and who weren't afraid to be authentic.

As the night wore on and we shared more stories and laughs, I realized how much my life had changed. I was no longer the person who needed constant validation from a faceless crowd. Instead, I had found a community where I could truly belong, where my worth wasn't measured by likes or comments but by the connections I made and the joy I found in the things I loved.

This new circle of friends became my anchor, grounding me as I continued to navigate the changes in my life. They reminded me that true fulfillment comes from within and from the relationships we build with those who share our values. It was a lesson I was grateful to have learned, and one that I knew would guide me as I continued on my journey of self-discovery.

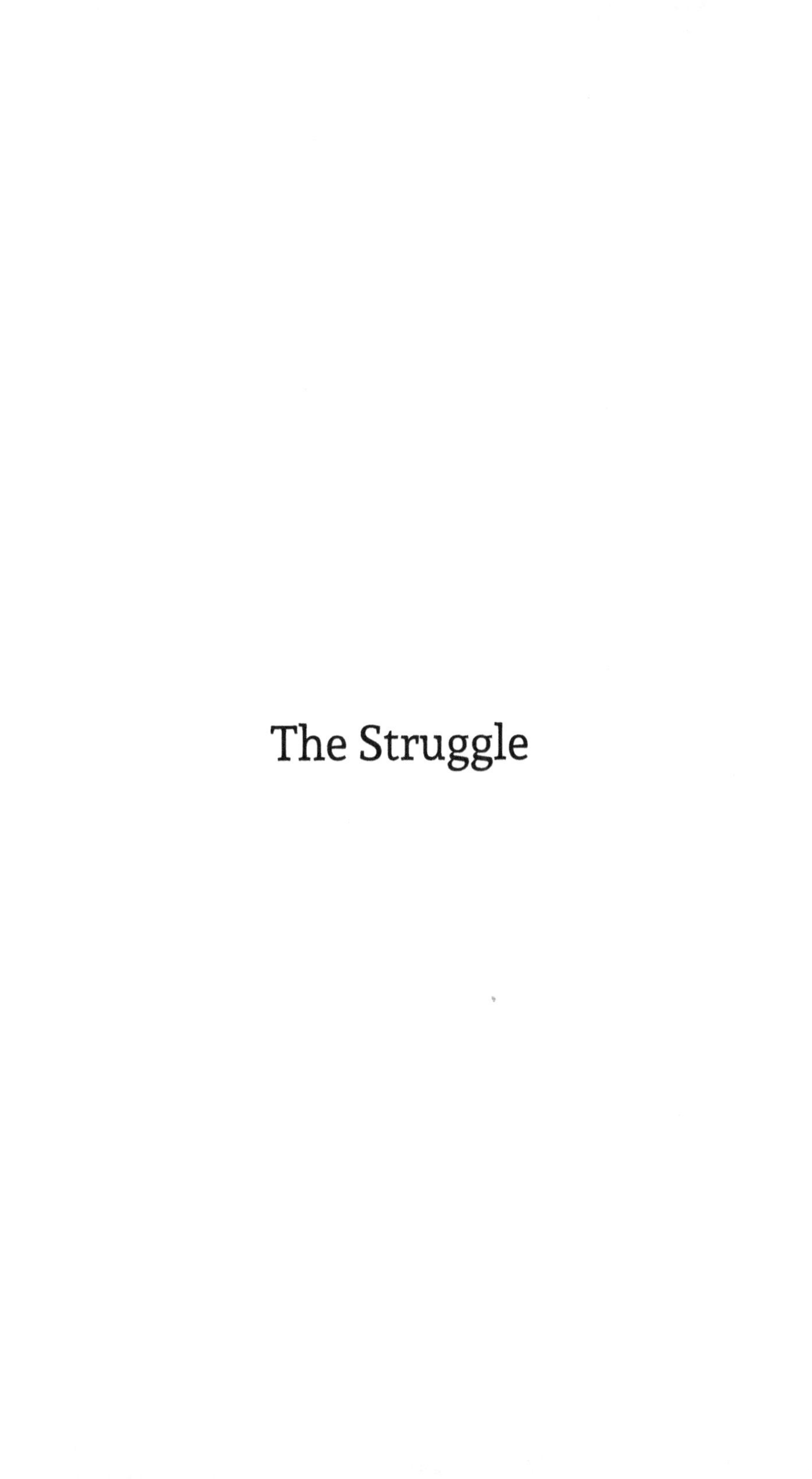

The Struggle

21

Temptation to Return

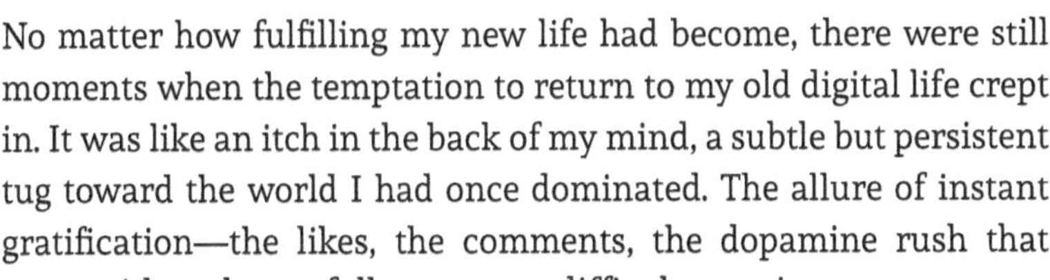

No matter how fulfilling my new life had become, there were still moments when the temptation to return to my old digital life crept in. It was like an itch in the back of my mind, a subtle but persistent tug toward the world I had once dominated. The allure of instant gratification—the likes, the comments, the dopamine rush that came with each new follower—was difficult to resist.

It often happened during quiet moments, when I was alone with my thoughts. I would be sitting in my room, strumming my guitar or editing photos from a recent walk, and suddenly, a wave of nostalgia would hit me. I would remember the thrill of going viral, the excitement of watching my follower count skyrocket, the way my phone would buzz with endless notifications. It was a powerful, intoxicating feeling, and it was hard to shake the memory of it.

One evening, after a particularly long day, I found myself scrolling through old photos on my phone—pictures from events, behind-the-scenes shots of my social media content, candid moments captured during my peak. My finger hovered over the Instagram app, and for a brief moment, I considered opening it, just to see what was happening.

Maybe I could just check in, I thought. Maybe I could post something small, something to remind everyone that I was still here. The idea was tempting—so easy, so immediate. I could feel the pull of that old life, the allure of the instant connection, the rush of validation.

But then I remembered what had come with it. The pressure, the anxiety, the constant need to perform and maintain an image that wasn't entirely true to who I was. I remembered the emptiness I had felt despite all the attention, the way it had drained me rather than fulfilled me.

I put my phone down and closed my eyes, taking a deep breath. The temptation was real, but so was the knowledge of where it had led me before. I had made a promise to myself, to Mia, to the new friends who had become my support system. I had promised to push forward with my journey, to find happiness and fulfillment in the real world, not in the fleeting moments of online fame.

The next morning, I decided to distract myself by diving deeper into my offline activities. I reached out to Rohan, asking if he was up for an impromptu photo walk. He agreed, and we spent the day exploring a part of the city neither of us had visited before. The conversations flowed easily, and I felt the familiar joy of being fully present in the moment, of capturing the world through my lens.

Later that day, I visited a local music store, one I had passed by many times but never entered. Inside, the smell of polished wood and the soft hum of acoustic guitars greeted me. I spent hours trying out different instruments, losing myself in the melodies and rhythms that had once been a core part of my life. It felt grounding, a reminder of the beauty that existed outside of the digital world.

But despite these efforts, the temptation still lingered. It wasn't something I could simply ignore or wish away. It was a struggle, a test of my resolve, and I knew that overcoming it required more than just distraction. It required a shift in perspective—a deeper understanding of why I had left that life behind in the first place.

One evening, I sat down with Mia, the person who had always been able to help me see things clearly. We were in the living room, a soft rain pattering against the windows, and I finally opened up to her about the struggle I was facing.

"I keep feeling this pull to go back," I admitted, my voice tinged with frustration. "It's like there's a part of me that still craves that validation, that attention. I know it's not good for me, but it's so hard to resist."

Mia listened quietly, her eyes filled with understanding. "It's natural to feel that way, Aryan. You spent so much time in that world—it's only normal that you'd miss parts of it. But you have to remember why you walked away. You weren't happy, even with all the fame and attention. It's like eating junk food—it might taste good in the moment, but it doesn't nourish you."

Her words struck a chord with me. I nodded, feeling the truth of what she was saying. "You're right. It's just hard to remind myself of that in the moment, you know? It's easy to get caught up in the idea of what it was like, without thinking about the reality."

"That's the challenge," Mia said gently. "But you've come so far, Aryan. You've started building a life that's based on real connections, on things that truly make you happy. Don't let the temptation pull you back into something that doesn't serve you. Keep focusing on what's real, what's meaningful."

Her encouragement gave me the strength I needed to keep pushing forward. I realized that the struggle wasn't just about resisting temptation; it was about choosing to prioritize the things that truly mattered in my life. It was about recognizing that the instant gratification of social media was a fleeting high, one that could never replace the deep, lasting fulfillment I was beginning to find in the offline world.

In the days that followed, I doubled down on my commitment to this new path. I made a conscious effort to stay engaged with my hobbies, to nurture my relationships, and to continue exploring the parts of life that brought me genuine joy. And each time the temptation to return to my old life reared its head, I reminded myself of the emptiness that had come with it—and of the richness that was now within my reach.

The journey wasn't easy, and the struggle was real, but with each passing day, I felt myself growing stronger, more grounded in the life I was building. The temptation to return would always be there, lurking in the background, but I knew now that I had the strength to push forward, to choose a path that truly nourished my soul.

22
The Social Media Detox

The decision to take a complete break from social media didn't come easily. For years, my life had revolved around the constant stream of updates, posts, and interactions. The idea of cutting myself off entirely felt daunting, almost unimaginable. But as the struggle to resist temptation grew, I knew that if I truly wanted to reclaim my life and identity, I had to take this step.

It started one evening after another moment of weakness where I found myself almost slipping back into old habits. I had picked up my phone, mindlessly scrolling through old notifications, and it hit me—this needed to stop. I needed a reset, a way to clear my mind and break the hold that social media still had on me. That night, I made the decision: a full detox, no social media, no lurking, no checking in.

I announced my departure with a final post—a simple message explaining that I was taking time away to focus on my well-being and find balance in my life. The response was immediate and overwhelming, with comments ranging from supportive wishes to confusion and concern. I turned off my notifications, deleted the apps from my phone, and logged out from all accounts. The silence that followed was both unsettling and oddly peaceful.

The first few days were the hardest. My fingers itched to check my phone, to open the apps that had been such a huge part of my daily routine. I felt a strange sense of emptiness, as if I were missing out on something vital. The anxiety was palpable—a nagging worry about what I was missing, what people were saying, and how my absence would be perceived. My mind kept drifting back to the thought of logging in, just for a moment, just to see.

But each time, I reminded myself why I was doing this. The detox wasn't just about stepping away from the digital world; it was about stepping back into the real one. I knew I had to endure the discomfort to reach the clarity and peace I was seeking.

To keep myself occupied, I threw myself into my offline interests. I spent hours taking photos, experimenting with new techniques and finding new subjects to capture. I lost myself in the world of music, learning new songs on the guitar and even attempting to write a few of my own. I also started journaling—a practice I hadn't engaged in for years. Writing down my thoughts, fears, and experiences provided an unexpected outlet, helping me process the emotions that surfaced during this period of withdrawal.

Gradually, the anxiety began to subside. The constant urge to check my phone lessened, and in its place, I started to feel something I hadn't felt in a long time—lightness. It was as if a weight had been lifted off my shoulders. The endless noise of social media had always been there, a constant hum in the background of my life, and now, in its absence, I was discovering a new kind of quiet, one that allowed me to think more clearly and feel more deeply.

With each passing day, the benefits of the detox became more apparent. I had more time to engage with the people around me, to truly listen and be present. I was more attuned to my surroundings, noticing the little details that I had previously overlooked in my rush to capture the perfect shot or craft the perfect post. The world seemed richer, more vibrant, and I was beginning to rediscover the joy of simply existing without the need to document or share every moment.

One evening, I found myself sitting by the lake, a place I had visited many times before, but this time it felt different. The water was calm, reflecting the golden hues of the setting sun. I sat there in silence, soaking in the beauty of the scene, and for the first time in a long while, I felt truly at peace. There was no need to capture this moment for anyone else; it was enough to experience it for myself.

The detox also gave me the space to confront some of the deeper issues I had been avoiding. Without the distraction of social media, I was forced to face the insecurities and fears that had driven my obsession with online validation. I realized how much I had relied on the opinions of others to define my self-worth and how that had led me down a path of emptiness and disconnection. This period of reflection was difficult, even painful at times, but it was necessary for my growth.

As the weeks went by, I began to feel a sense of freedom that I hadn't experienced in years. The pressure to perform, to be constantly visible and relevant, had dissipated. I no longer felt the need to compare myself to others or to measure my success by the number of likes or followers. Instead, I was finding fulfillment in the small, everyday moments—things that were genuine and meaningful, untainted by the need for external approval.

The detox wasn't just a break from social media; it was a journey back to myself. I was rediscovering who I was without the filter of my online persona, reconnecting with my true passions, and rebuilding my sense of self-worth from the inside out. It wasn't always easy, but it was the most important thing I could have done for myself.

As the detox period came to an end, I knew I had changed. The allure of social media was still there, but it no longer held the same power over me. I had learned to value the real world—the connections, the experiences, and the peace that came with being present. I wasn't sure what the future held or how I would navigate my online presence moving forward, but one thing was clear: I was no longer defined by it. I had found a way to be truly free.

23
Discovering Real Friendships

The more time I spent with my new friends, the more I realized just how different these relationships were from the ones I had formed online. It was like stepping into a world that I hadn't fully understood before—a world where friendship wasn't measured in likes, comments, or shares, but in the depth of connection, the joy of shared experiences, and the simple act of being there for one another.

It started gradually, as I continued to meet up with Rohan, Neha, and the rest of the photography group. What had initially been casual outings to explore the city and take pictures evolved into something much more meaningful. We began to spend time together outside of our scheduled meet-ups—grabbing coffee, having long conversations over dinner, and even organizing weekend trips to nearby towns for a change of scenery.

One Saturday, after a particularly intense day of shooting in a bustling market, Rohan suggested we all head to his place to relax and unwind. The idea was appealing, so we piled into cars and made our way to his apartment. What followed was a night filled with laughter, music, and the kind of conversations that seem to flow endlessly when you're surrounded by people who truly get you.

As we sat around Rohan's living room, the sound of an acoustic guitar playing softly in the background, I felt a warmth in my chest—a feeling of comfort and belonging that I hadn't experienced in a long time. This was different from the carefully curated moments I used to share online. There was no need to perform or to present a perfect version of myself. I could just be, and that was enough.

At one point, Neha leaned over and asked, "So, Aryan, what's the story behind your love for photography? You've got a real eye for it, but I feel like there's more to it than just a hobby."

Her question caught me off guard. I hadn't really talked about why I'd started taking photos in the first place, especially not with the people I'd met online. It had always been about creating content, chasing trends, and gaining followers. But here, with these friends, I felt safe enough to open up.

"I guess it started as a way to capture memories," I began, choosing my words carefully. "When I was younger, my family used to take a lot of trips—road trips, vacations, you name it. My dad had this old camera, and he'd let me use it sometimes. I loved how I could freeze a moment in time, something I could look back on and remember exactly how I felt. But somewhere along the way, I lost that. Photography became more about getting the perfect shot for Instagram, about impressing people rather than capturing what mattered to me."

Rohan nodded thoughtfully. "I get that. It's easy to lose sight of why we start doing something when there's so much pressure to turn it into content."

"Yeah," I agreed. "But since I've stepped back from social media, I've been trying to reconnect with that original feeling, to find the joy in it again. And I think being with you guys, seeing how you approach photography, has helped me do that."

Neha smiled warmly. "We're glad to have you with us, Aryan. It's clear that you've got a passion for this, and it's been amazing to see how you've grown since we first met."

Her words meant more to me than she probably realized. These friendships weren't just about the things we did together—they were about the way we supported and encouraged each other, the way we shared our struggles and triumphs without judgment or expectation. It was a far cry from the shallow, transactional relationships I'd had online, where connections were often based on mutual benefit rather than genuine care.

Over the next few weeks, I found myself spending more and more time with this group. We'd have spontaneous get-togethers, go on road trips, and even plan creative projects that had nothing to do with social media. There was a sense of ease and freedom in these interactions that I hadn't known I was missing. We could talk for hours, or just sit in comfortable silence, knowing that the connection didn't need to be constantly affirmed or validated.

One evening, we decided to have a bonfire at a nearby beach. As the flames crackled and the sun dipped below the horizon, we shared stories, roasted marshmallows, and played music. I found myself reflecting on how far I had come since I started this journey of rediscovery. The friendships I was building now were real—rooted in mutual respect, shared interests, and a deep sense of trust.

Mia, who had come along for the bonfire, pulled me aside as we were packing up to leave. "You seem different, Aryan," she said, her eyes searching mine. "Happier, more at peace."

I smiled, realizing she was right. "I think I am. These friendships...they're real, Mia. They're not based on what I can offer or what people think of me. They're based on who I am, and that's something I haven't felt in a long time."

"I'm glad," she said, squeezing my hand. "You deserve this. You deserve to be surrounded by people who care about you for you."

As we walked back to the car, the last embers of the bonfire glowing softly in the distance, I felt a renewed sense of purpose and belonging. The friendships I was discovering weren't just filling the void that social media had left behind—they were enriching my life in ways I hadn't anticipated. They were helping me to rediscover who I was, not just as a creator or an influencer, but as a person—a friend, a companion, someone who had value beyond the digital realm.

For the first time in a long while, I felt like I was truly living. These real friendships were the foundation of a new chapter in my life, one that was defined not by the superficial metrics of the online world, but by the depth of connection and the joy of shared experiences. I knew now that this was where I belonged, and it was a feeling I intended to hold onto with everything I had.

24
The Unveiling of the Mystery Messenger

The messages had started appearing a few weeks after I began my journey of self-discovery, just as I was beginning to distance myself from the digital world. They were always brief, almost cryptic—small reminders to stay grounded, to remember who I was beneath the persona I had created online. At first, I dismissed them as the work of a well-meaning fan, someone who had noticed my recent struggles and wanted to offer encouragement from afar. But as the weeks passed, I couldn't shake the feeling that there was something more to it.

The messages always arrived at the right moment, when I needed them most. They appeared in my email, my DMs, even as handwritten notes left at places I frequented—coffee shops, the photography studio, even tucked into the pages of a book I had borrowed from Rohan. They were a lifeline during the hardest moments, a quiet voice of reason when I was tempted to fall back into old habits.

But who was behind them? And why had they chosen to reach out in this way, shrouded in mystery?

One evening, after returning from a particularly fulfilling day spent with my new friends, I found a note slipped under my door. The handwriting was familiar now, and I felt a strange mixture of anticipation and anxiety as I unfolded the paper. It was a simple message, just like the others, but this time, it included something new—a time and a place: "It's time we met. Tomorrow at 5 PM, the café where it all started."

My heart raced as I reread the note. The café where it all started—the one where I had first begun meeting with other content creators, where I had planned my rise to fame. The place held a lot of memories, both good and bad, and now, it seemed, it would be the site of another significant moment in my life.

The next day, I arrived at the café early, my mind swirling with possibilities. Who could it be? An old friend? A former collaborator? I ordered a coffee and chose a table near the back, away from the bustling crowds. The minutes ticked by slowly, each one heightening my anticipation.

At exactly 5 PM, the door opened, and I watched as someone I hadn't seen in years walked in. It was Aarav—a close friend from my school days, someone who had known me long before the world of social media had taken over my life. We had been inseparable back then, spending countless hours talking about our dreams, our plans for the future. But as I got swept up in the digital world, we had drifted apart, losing touch as my focus shifted to my online persona.

"Aarav?" I said, standing up, a mix of shock and disbelief in my voice. "Is it really you?"

He smiled, a little sheepishly, and nodded. "Yeah, it's me. Surprised?"

"More than surprised," I admitted, gesturing for him to sit down. "I...I didn't expect it to be you. How did you...why did you...?"

He sighed, running a hand through his hair as he looked at me with a mixture of concern and affection. "I've been watching from a distance, Aryan. Watching you rise to fame, but also watching you lose yourself in it. I tried reaching out a few times, but it felt like you were slipping further away. I didn't know how to get through to you, and I was afraid you wouldn't listen, so I thought maybe this would work."

"You were the one sending the messages?" I asked, still processing the revelation. "All this time, it was you?"

"Yeah," he admitted, his voice soft. "I knew you were going through something, and I wanted to help, but I didn't know how to do it directly. I hoped the messages would at least make you think, make you pause and remember who you are. I wanted to remind you of the things that really matter."

His words hit me hard. This whole time, it had been Aarav, someone who had known me before the fame, before the pressures of social media had changed me. He had seen me for who I truly was and had wanted to help me find my way back.

"I don't know what to say," I said, emotion welling up inside me. "I'm so sorry, Aarav. For losing touch, for not being there...I got so caught up in everything that I forgot about the people who really mattered. You were right, I lost myself. And if it weren't for those messages, I don't know if I would have ever realized it."

He shook his head, his expression kind. "You don't have to apologize, Aryan. I know how easy it is to get lost in that world. I just wanted to make sure you didn't lose yourself completely. And look at you now—you're finding your way back."

I felt a deep sense of gratitude toward Aarav. He had cared enough to reach out, to keep reminding me of who I was, even when I didn't see it myself. His actions had been selfless, driven by a genuine concern for my well-being, and now, sitting across from him, I realized how much I had missed having him in my life.

"Thank you," I said, my voice thick with emotion. "Thank you for not giving up on me, for being there when I needed it most, even if I didn't know it."

He smiled, his eyes reflecting the warmth of our old friendship. "That's what friends are for, right? And besides, I missed you too. It wasn't easy watching you go through all that, but I knew you had the strength to find your way back. I'm just glad I could be there to help."

We spent the next few hours catching up, reminiscing about the old days, and talking about everything that had happened since we last saw each other. It was a cathartic experience, one that helped me put the pieces of my life into perspective. Aarav's presence reminded me of the person I had been before social media had taken over—a person who valued deep connections, who cared about the people in his life, who wanted to make a difference in the world, not just online.

As we parted ways that evening, I felt a renewed sense of resolve. Aarav's revelation had given me the clarity I needed to stay on this new path, to continue distancing myself from the toxic elements of the digital world, and to focus on the things that truly mattered—real friendships, genuine experiences, and a life lived with purpose.

The mystery messenger was no longer a mystery, but a cherished friend who had guided me back to myself. And as I walked away from the café, I knew that this was just the beginning of a new chapter in my life—one where I could finally be the person I was meant to be, with the support of those who truly cared about me.

25
Family Reconciliation

With each passing day, as I delved deeper into my journey of self-discovery, one truth became increasingly clear: I couldn't fully move forward without addressing the rift that had grown between me and my family. For years, I had been so consumed by the digital world that I had allowed my most important relationships to wither. It was time to change that.

I started small. One morning, instead of scrolling through my phone as I usually did, I made breakfast for everyone. It was a simple gesture, but as I set the table and called out to my parents and siblings, I realized how long it had been since we had shared a meal together. The awkwardness was palpable at first—my father gave me a puzzled look, my mother seemed hesitant, and my siblings were unsure how to react. But as we sat down and the smell of fresh pancakes filled the room, something shifted. We talked, though the conversation was light and mostly about everyday things, it was a start.

Over the next few weeks, I made a conscious effort to spend more time at home. I joined my parents for evening tea, helped my younger brother with his homework, and even offered to cook dinner with my mother, a task I hadn't done in years. Each of these moments, while seemingly small, was a step toward rebuilding the connections I had let slip away.

One weekend, I suggested we go on a family outing, something we hadn't done in ages. To my surprise, everyone agreed, albeit with a bit of reluctance. We chose a nearby park, a place we used to visit when I was younger. As we walked together, the atmosphere was lighter than it had been in a long time. My father and I talked about his work, my mother shared stories about her childhood, and my siblings laughed and joked with each other. It felt almost like old times, and I couldn't help but smile at the realization that these moments were what I had been missing all along.

But the process of reconciliation wasn't without its challenges. There were moments when old tensions resurfaced, especially when it came to the choices I had made during my rise to fame. My father, who had always been supportive yet cautious about my social media career, brought up the distance it had created between us. "You know, Aryan," he said one evening as we sat on the porch, "I always wondered if you saw what was happening. We were proud of your success, but it felt like we were losing you in the process."

His words stung, but I knew they were true. "I did lose myself," I admitted, looking out at the fading sunset. "And in the process, I lost touch with what really matters. I'm sorry, Dad. I should have been more present, more aware."

He nodded, placing a hand on my shoulder. "What matters is that you're here now, trying to make things right. That takes courage."

Our conversation marked a turning point. From that moment on, there was a renewed effort from both sides to rebuild our relationship. I started opening up more, sharing not just the good moments but also the struggles I had faced. My mother, who had always been the emotional anchor of the family, listened with understanding and offered her support in a way that only she could.

One evening, as we sat together in the living room, my sister, who had been the most distant of all, finally broke her silence. "I was angry at you," she confessed, her voice trembling slightly. "You were always so busy, always somewhere else, and I felt like I didn't matter to you anymore."

Her words hit me hard. "You did matter," I said softly. "You always did. I just...I lost sight of what was important. But I'm here now, and I want to make it right."

She nodded, tears welling up in her eyes. "I know. I can see you're trying, and that means a lot."

We hugged, a gesture that seemed to break down the final barrier between us. It was as if we were finally acknowledging the pain that had been buried for so long and deciding to move forward together.

The process of reconciliation was gradual, with ups and downs along the way, but each day brought us closer. We began to rediscover the joy of simply being a family—playing board games, watching movies together, and even planning a weekend getaway. It wasn't perfect, but it was real, and that was enough.

As I spent more time with my family, I felt a deep sense of connection to my roots. I realized that my identity wasn't just tied to the online persona I had created, but to the values and experiences that had shaped me growing up. My family had always been my foundation, and it was time I started treating them as such.

Looking back, I understood that this journey wasn't just about distancing myself from the digital world—it was about reconnecting with the people who had always been there, waiting for me to return. And with each passing day, I felt more at peace, more grounded in the things that truly mattered. I was no longer just Aryan, the social media influencer—I was Aryan, the son, the brother, the friend. And that was a role I was finally ready to embrace fully.

26
Facing the Critics

It was inevitable that my decision to step back from the digital world would draw attention. At first, I expected the criticism—after all, the influencer world thrived on controversy and drama. But even with that expectation, the backlash still hit harder than I anticipated.

The comments began trickling in slowly, a few here and there under my older posts. "Where did the real Aryan go?" one asked, laced with sarcasm. "Looks like fame got too much for him," another sniped. Then there were the direct messages from followers who felt betrayed. They accused me of abandoning them, of letting them down just when they needed me most. I even received messages from other influencers, some I had considered friends, who hinted that I had lost my edge, that my relevance was slipping away.

It was strange, standing on the outside looking in. For so long, I had been wrapped up in the whirlwind of online validation, feeding off the likes, shares, and comments as if they were my lifeblood. Now, seeing how quickly the tide had turned, I felt a mixture of sadness and relief. Sadness because I knew these reactions came from a place of disappointment or confusion—people didn't understand the changes I was going through. And relief because I was no longer chained to the expectations of others.

One evening, I decided to go through the comments more thoroughly. I needed to face what was being said, to confront the reality of how my absence was perceived. Some were just mean-spirited, full of the kind of negativity that thrived in the online world. But others came from genuine confusion, a feeling of betrayal that I hadn't anticipated. These people had followed me for years, watching my every move, and to them, my sudden detachment felt like a betrayal. They had invested in my life, and now, they didn't know what to make of the new direction I was taking.

But I knew this wasn't just about me. The harshest critics often revealed more about themselves than they did about the person they were criticizing. The influencer world was a competitive space, filled with people who were constantly striving to maintain their status, their relevance. My decision to step away challenged the very foundation of that world. To some, it was a sign of weakness, of giving up. To others, it was an affront, as if my departure cast a shadow on their own choices.

There were also those who saw my journey as a threat to the carefully curated image they had of me. I was no longer the person they had idolized, the one who lived a seemingly perfect life in front of the camera. I was now someone who was questioning the very life that had brought me fame, and that made people uncomfortable. My change was a mirror, reflecting back the insecurities and doubts they might have had about their own lives.

Despite the noise, I stood firm. I had made a conscious choice to prioritize my mental health, my relationships, and my well-being over the fleeting satisfaction of online validation. And no amount of criticism could change the clarity I had gained in the process. I no longer needed the approval of others to feel secure in my decisions. What mattered most was how I felt about myself and the direction I was heading.

To remind myself of why I started this journey, I revisited the moments that had led me here. The exhaustion, the feeling of emptiness despite the adoration, the realization that my life had become a performance—all of it reinforced my decision. I thought about the conversation with Aarav, the time spent reconnecting with my family, the sense of fulfillment I found in my offline hobbies. These were the things that truly mattered, the things that gave my life meaning.

Still, the criticism wasn't easy to brush off. There were days when the negativity got to me, when I wondered if I was making a mistake by turning my back on the life I had built. But every time those doubts crept in, I reminded myself of the emptiness that had come with chasing likes and followers, the void that no amount of online praise could fill.

One day, after a particularly tough session of reading through comments, I decided to respond—not to defend myself, but to offer some clarity. I composed a post, carefully choosing my words to reflect my truth.

"I know many of you are wondering why I've been distant, why I'm not the same Aryan you've come to know over the years. The truth is, I've changed. I realized that the life I was living wasn't sustainable, that it was taking more from me than it was giving. I needed to step back, to rediscover who I am outside of this digital world. This journey isn't about abandoning anyone—it's about finding myself again. I hope you can understand that."

The response was mixed, as I expected. Some appreciated the honesty, while others saw it as an excuse. But that was okay. I wasn't looking for validation; I just wanted to be transparent about where I stood.

As the days passed, the criticism began to lose its sting. I realized that I didn't have to carry the weight of others' expectations. My journey was mine alone, and it was okay if not everyone understood it. What mattered most was that I was finally living a life that felt authentic, a life where I didn't have to perform for anyone.

The criticism would always be there, lurking in the background, but I had made peace with it. I was no longer the Aryan who needed constant validation from the outside world. I was someone who had found strength in vulnerability, who had learned that it was okay to change, to grow, to prioritize myself.

And with that, I continued forward, more determined than ever to stay true to the path I had chosen, no matter what anyone else had to say about it.

27
The Joy of Privacy

For as long as I could remember, my life had been an open book—a carefully curated narrative shared with millions of strangers on the internet. Every meal, every trip, every moment of success and failure had been documented, filtered, and presented to the world. Privacy was a concept I had long forgotten, sacrificed on the altar of likes, shares, and comments. But now, as I stepped further away from the digital spotlight, I began to rediscover the profound joy of privacy.

It started subtly, like a warm breeze after a long, cold winter. The first time I noticed it was during a quiet afternoon at home. I was sitting by the window, a cup of tea in hand, watching the world go by outside. There was no camera pointed at me, no phone in my hand ready to capture the moment. It was just me, alone with my thoughts, completely present in the moment. I took a deep breath, and for the first time in years, I felt an overwhelming sense of peace.

Privacy had become a luxury, something I hadn't even realized I was missing. There was a beauty in living life away from the prying eyes of others, in experiencing moments that belonged solely to me and the people I chose to share them with. No longer was I living under the constant pressure to present a version of myself that was palatable to the masses. Instead, I was free to be unapologetically myself, flaws and all.

I began to cherish the little things that once seemed mundane but now held a new significance. Morning walks became a time for reflection, where I could enjoy the crisp air and the sound of birds without worrying about capturing the perfect shot for Instagram. Meals with my family were no longer interrupted by the need to document every dish—I could simply enjoy the food and the company without any distractions. Even the act of reading a book felt different, more intimate, now that it was a private pleasure rather than content to be shared.

The more I embraced my newfound privacy, the more I realized how much I had missed out on in my pursuit of online fame. I had traded genuine connection for superficial engagement, real moments for manufactured ones. But now, as I reclaimed my life from the digital world, I felt like I was finally living in the present, fully engaged with the people and experiences around me.

One of the most surprising aspects of this journey was how it deepened my relationships. Without the constant intrusion of social media, I was able to connect with my family and friends on a much more personal level. Conversations became more meaningful when they weren't being broadcasted to the world. I could confide in someone without worrying about how it would be perceived by others or how it might affect my online persona. Trust became the foundation of my relationships, rather than the approval of strangers.

I also noticed how much lighter I felt, both mentally and emotionally. The constant need to maintain an image, to be always "on," had been exhausting in ways I hadn't fully acknowledged. Now, without that burden, I found myself more at ease, more content with who I was. I no longer needed to seek validation from outside sources; instead, I found fulfillment in the quiet, private moments that were mine alone.

Privacy gave me the space to explore my thoughts and emotions without judgment. I began journaling again, something I hadn't done since before my rise to fame. In the pages of my journal, I could be completely honest with myself, processing my experiences and emotions in a way that felt safe and authentic. It was a form of self-care that I had long neglected, and it helped me to gain clarity and insight into who I was becoming.

As the days turned into weeks, I started to embrace the idea that not everything needed to be shared. There was power in keeping some parts of my life to myself, in holding onto moments that were sacred and personal. It was a form of self-preservation, a way to protect the peace and happiness I had worked so hard to achieve.

Of course, the temptation to share was still there, especially when something exciting or beautiful happened. But each time, I reminded myself of the joy I had found in privacy, in living a life that was mine alone. I no longer needed the approval of others to validate my experiences. The thrill of sharing had been replaced by the deeper, more lasting satisfaction of simply living.

In time, I noticed how this shift in perspective affected the way I saw the world. I became more observant, more appreciative of the small details that I once overlooked in my rush to capture the big picture. The world seemed richer, more vibrant, when I wasn't viewing it through the lens of a camera or the screen of a phone. I was finally seeing life for what it was, in all its messy, beautiful, and unpredictable glory.

And in this new reality, I found a peace that I hadn't known I was missing. It wasn't the fleeting, surface-level peace that came from a successful post or a surge in followers. It was a deep, enduring peace that came from within, from knowing that I was living authentically, on my own terms.

The joy of privacy was something I had to learn to value again, but now that I had, I knew it was something I would never willingly give up. I was no longer Aryan, the influencer whose life was on display for the world to see. I was simply Aryan, a person who had rediscovered the beauty of living a life that was truly his own. And in that privacy, I found a happiness that no amount of fame could ever bring.

28
Newfound Passions

The more time I spent away from the constant buzz of social media, the more I realized how much I had been missing. My life had been so consumed by likes, comments, and shares that I had forgotten the simple joy of exploring new interests, of finding passions that could bring me true fulfillment. As I ventured further into this new chapter of my life, I began to rediscover old hobbies and, to my delight, uncover new ones.

It started with a spontaneous decision to travel. For years, my trips had been meticulously planned with content creation in mind—every location, every meal, every experience carefully curated to produce the perfect shot. But this time, I wanted something different. I booked a ticket to a small town I had never heard of, somewhere off the beaten path, with no agenda other than to explore.

The trip was a revelation. Without the pressure of documenting every moment, I was free to truly immerse myself in the experience. I wandered through quiet streets, talked to locals, and let myself get lost in the beauty of my surroundings. The world felt vast and full of possibilities in a way it hadn't for a long time. I wasn't thinking about how to present this to others; I was simply enjoying it for myself. The mountains, the rivers, the simple pleasure of sitting in a quaint café with a good book—these were moments that filled me with a sense of peace and wonder I hadn't known I was missing.

As I traveled more, I felt a growing desire to capture these experiences—not for an audience, but for myself. I picked up my old camera, a tool I had once loved but had neglected in favor of my phone. Photography had been a passion of mine long before I became an influencer, and now, without the pressure to perform, I found myself falling in love with it all over again. The world looked different through the lens of a camera, more textured and nuanced. Each photograph I took felt like a personal keepsake, a memory preserved in time just for me.

But photography wasn't the only passion that reemerged during this period of exploration. I also found myself drawn back to writing, something I hadn't done seriously in years. I started journaling regularly, capturing my thoughts, feelings, and observations in a way that felt raw and honest. Writing became a form of therapy, a way to process the changes I was going through and to make sense of the new direction my life was taking. Soon, journaling wasn't enough, and I began experimenting with short stories, essays, and even poetry. Each piece I wrote was a reflection of my journey, a way to express the thoughts and emotions that were bubbling up inside me.

As I continued to write, I realized that this wasn't just a hobby—it was a passion that had been lying dormant, overshadowed by the noise of my digital life. There was something profoundly satisfying about putting pen to paper (or fingers to keyboard) and creating something purely for the joy of creation. Writing gave me a voice that was entirely my own, unfiltered by the expectations of an online audience. It was freeing, and it brought me a sense of fulfillment that I hadn't felt in years.

And then, there was art. Growing up, I had always loved to draw, to paint, to create with my hands. But as my online presence grew, I had pushed those creative urges aside, telling myself I didn't have time for them. Now, with my newfound freedom, I found myself drawn back to the world of art. I started small—sketching in a notebook, experimenting with watercolors—but soon, I was spending hours lost in the act of creation. Art became a meditative practice, a way to express the inexpressible, to explore emotions that words couldn't capture.

Each new passion I discovered felt like a piece of myself falling back into place, filling the void that social media had once occupied. I was no longer chasing after the fleeting satisfaction of likes and shares; instead, I was pursuing the things that brought me genuine joy and fulfillment. Traveling, writing, art—these passions were more than just hobbies; they were a path back to myself, a way to reconnect with the person I had been before the allure of fame had taken over my life.

As I embraced these newfound passions, I began to see the world differently. Life felt richer, more vibrant, full of endless possibilities. There was so much to explore, so much to experience, and for the first time in a long time, I was excited about the future. I no longer felt the need to broadcast every achievement, to seek validation from others. The joy I found in these activities was enough.

What surprised me most was how these passions began to influence other areas of my life. My creativity seeped into everything I did, from the way I approached challenges to how I connected with others. I felt more present, more engaged with the world around me. The more I pursued these interests, the more I realized that this was what I had been searching for all along—a life that was meaningful, fulfilling, and entirely my own.

In the past, my identity had been tied to my online persona, to the carefully crafted image I presented to the world. But now, as I explored these new passions, I was discovering a deeper, more authentic sense of self. I was no longer defined by the numbers on a screen; I was defined by the things that truly mattered to me, the things that brought me joy and fulfillment.

And with that realization came a profound sense of peace. I didn't need to return to the life I had left behind. I was forging a new path, one that was guided by my passions and interests, rather than the expectations of others. This was the life I wanted to live, a life where every day was an opportunity to learn, to grow, to create.

As I continued on this journey, I knew there would be challenges, moments of doubt, and temptation to revert to old habits. But I also knew that I had found something worth holding onto—a sense of purpose and fulfillment that couldn't be measured by likes or followers. I was no longer chasing after an elusive sense of happiness. Instead, I was living it, one day at a time, with each new passion guiding me further along the path to my true self.

29
The Challenge of Balance

Leaving my old life behind hadn't been as simple as flipping a switch. The decision to step away from the constant demands of social media had brought me peace and fulfillment I hadn't known I was missing. Yet, as time passed, I realized that the digital world wasn't something I could entirely escape. It was everywhere—in work, in communication, in the way people interacted with the world around them. The challenge now wasn't just in letting go but in finding a way to coexist with it without falling back into old patterns.

The truth was, social media wasn't inherently bad. It had connected me with people, allowed me to share my passions, and even provided me with opportunities that I never would have had otherwise. The problem had been in my relationship with it, in the way I had allowed it to consume me, to dictate my self-worth and sense of identity. Now, as I moved forward, I knew I needed to find a balance, a way to stay connected without losing myself again.

The first step in this journey was recognizing my triggers. I knew that certain aspects of social media—like the constant need for validation, the endless scrolling, the comparison with others—had been toxic for me. So, I made a conscious effort to avoid those pitfalls. I set limits on my screen time, unfollowed accounts that made me feel inadequate, and turned off notifications that once had me checking my phone every few minutes. These small changes made a big difference, giving me the space to engage with social media on my terms, rather than being controlled by it.

But the real challenge was deeper than just managing my time online. It was about redefining my relationship with social media, finding a way to use it as a tool rather than allowing it to use me. I started by being more intentional with my online presence. Instead of mindlessly sharing every aspect of my life, I chose to share only what felt authentic and meaningful. My posts became less frequent, but more genuine, reflecting the person I was becoming rather than the persona I had created.

I also began to explore new ways to connect with others that didn't rely on likes and comments. I reached out to friends and family through phone calls and face-to-face meetings, valuing real conversations over virtual interactions. It felt good to reconnect with people on a more personal level, to have discussions that weren't interrupted by the need to document them for an audience. These interactions reminded me of the value of genuine connection, something that had often been lost in the noise of social media.

However, balancing my online and offline life wasn't always easy. There were times when the temptation to return to my old habits was strong, especially when I saw others thriving in the digital world. I would catch myself wondering if I was missing out, if my choice to step back was holding me back from opportunities or recognition. But each time, I reminded myself of the emptiness I had felt when I was fully immersed in that world. The validation it offered was fleeting, and the cost to my mental and emotional well-being was too high.

To help maintain this balance, I set clear boundaries for myself. I allocated specific times of the day for social media use, making sure it didn't encroach on the things that truly mattered to me—my passions, my relationships, and my personal growth. I also made a point to take regular breaks, stepping away from the screen entirely when I felt it was starting to take over. These boundaries weren't always easy to enforce, but they were necessary for me to stay true to the path I had chosen.

As I navigated this new relationship with social media, I began to notice a shift in my perspective. Instead of seeing it as a place where I had to compete or perform, I started to view it as a tool for connection and creativity. I found ways to use my platform to share the things that genuinely excited me—my photography, my writing, my travels—without getting caught up in the metrics. It was liberating to create content that wasn't driven by the need for approval but by my passion for the things I loved.

I also learned to embrace the idea of digital minimalism. I simplified my online presence, focusing on quality over quantity. I curated my feed to include only what inspired me, what brought me joy, or what genuinely mattered to me. This approach made my time online more meaningful and less overwhelming. I wasn't bombarded with endless content that left me feeling drained or dissatisfied; instead, I was engaging with things that added value to my life.

One of the most important lessons I learned during this time was the importance of mindfulness. I became more aware of how I felt before, during, and after using social media. If I noticed that I was starting to feel anxious, inadequate, or disconnected, I knew it was time to take a step back. By being mindful of my emotions, I was better able to manage my relationship with social media and prevent it from becoming a negative influence in my life.

In the end, finding balance was about being honest with myself. I had to acknowledge that social media would always be a part of my life, but it didn't have to define me. It could be a tool for connection and creativity, but only if I used it in a way that was healthy and aligned with my values. This meant being vigilant, setting boundaries, and constantly reassessing my relationship with it.

As I continued on this journey, I realized that balance wasn't a destination but a process. It required ongoing effort, self-awareness, and a commitment to my well-being. There would be times when I would falter, when the pull of my old life would tempt me to return. But I also knew that I had the strength to stay true to the path I had chosen, to continue building a life that was meaningful, fulfilling, and authentically mine.

In finding this balance, I discovered a new sense of freedom. I was no longer a prisoner to the digital world, nor was I trying to escape it entirely. I was simply learning to live with it in a way that supported my happiness and growth. And in that balance, I found a peace that allowed me to fully embrace the life I was creating—one that was rooted in real connections, genuine passions, and a deep understanding of who I truly was.

30
The New Normal

As the months passed, I found myself settling into a rhythm that felt both unfamiliar and strangely comforting—a new normal, one where my life was no longer dictated by the incessant demands of social media. This transition didn't happen overnight, nor was it without its challenges, but as I embraced this new chapter, I discovered a sense of contentment and peace that had long eluded me.

Gone were the days when I woke up reaching for my phone, eager to check notifications, to see how many likes my latest post had garnered, or to measure my success by the numbers on a screen. Instead, my mornings began with quiet moments of reflection, with the simple pleasures of a cup of coffee, a walk outside, or the pages of a good book. I had reclaimed these moments for myself, and they became a cherished part of my daily routine, grounding me in the present and setting a calm tone for the day ahead.

Social media still had a place in my life, but it was no longer the central focus. I used it sparingly, as a tool for connection rather than a source of validation. My posts became less frequent but more meaningful, reflecting the life I was now living rather than the one I had once curated for public consumption. I shared moments that genuinely mattered to me—an evening spent with friends, a photo from a recent trip, a piece of writing I was proud of—without the pressure to perform or impress.

The more I embraced this new normal, the more I realized how much I had been missing before. Without the constant noise of social media, I had space to breathe, to think, to explore the things that truly brought me joy. My offline passions flourished, filling my days with activities that were deeply fulfilling. Whether it was photography, writing, or simply spending time with loved ones, these pursuits gave my life a richness and depth that no amount of online recognition could ever replicate.

I also noticed a shift in my relationships. The connections I formed now were built on mutual respect, trust, and shared experiences, rather than the superficial bonds that had once dominated my social media interactions. I found myself surrounded by people who valued me for who I was, not for the persona I had created online. These friendships brought a sense of belonging and support that had been absent in my previous life, and I treasured them deeply.

Of course, there were still moments when I felt the pull of my old life. The allure of instant gratification, the temptation to check in on what I was missing, the occasional pang of insecurity when I saw others thriving in the digital world—these feelings didn't disappear entirely. But each time they surfaced, I reminded myself of the emptiness that had come with that life, of the peace I had found in stepping away from it. I had learned to navigate these moments with mindfulness and self-compassion, understanding that they were part of the journey, not a sign of failure.

In this new normal, I also became more aware of the impact I could have online. I was no longer interested in chasing fame or followers, but I still wanted to use my platform in a way that aligned with my values. I started sharing content that was authentic and purposeful, that reflected the lessons I had learned and the life I was now living. Whether it was a thoughtful reflection, a creative project, or a simple message of kindness, I wanted my online presence to contribute something positive to the world.

This mindful approach to social media brought a sense of balance that had been missing before. I no longer felt the need to document every moment or to constantly be plugged in. Instead, I used social media in a way that enhanced my life rather than detracting from it. It became a space where I could connect with friends, share meaningful moments, and express myself creatively, without the pressure to conform to external expectations.

As I settled into this new normal, I found a contentment that was both surprising and deeply satisfying. My life was no longer defined by the opinions of others or by the number of likes and followers I had. Instead, it was shaped by the things that truly mattered to me—my passions, my relationships, my personal growth. I had discovered a way to integrate social media into my life without letting it take over, and in doing so, I had found a sense of peace that I hadn't known was possible.

Looking back, I realized how far I had come. The journey hadn't been easy, and there had been moments when I had questioned whether I was making the right choices. But as I stood in this new place, with a life that felt rich, meaningful, and authentically mine, I knew that every step had been worth it. I had reclaimed my sense of self, and in doing so, I had created a life that was not only sustainable but deeply fulfilling.

This new normal wasn't about rejecting technology or turning my back on the digital world. It was about finding a way to coexist with it, to use it as a tool rather than a crutch, and to live a life that was rooted in reality rather than performance. It was about balance, about knowing when to engage and when to step back, and about prioritizing the things that truly brought me happiness.

In the end, I had found what I had been searching for all along—not in the fleeting highs of social media fame, but in the quiet, steady rhythm of a life well-lived. This new normal was my own, and it was enough.

The Transformation

31

Redefining Success

As I ventured deeper into this new chapter of my life, I realized that the concept of success, something I had once obsessed over, needed to be reexamined. For so long, success had been synonymous with followers, likes, and lucrative brand deals. It was a definition shaped by the digital world, one that rewarded visibility and external validation above all else. But as I distanced myself from that world, I began to see how narrow and unfulfilling that definition truly was.

The more I reflected on my journey, the more I understood that success wasn't a one-size-fits-all concept. It wasn't about meeting society's expectations or achieving milestones that others deemed important. Instead, success was deeply personal, something that had to be defined on my own terms, according to what brought me genuine happiness and fulfillment.

This redefinition of success was liberating in a way I hadn't anticipated. It freed me from the relentless pursuit of numbers and recognition, allowing me to focus on the things that truly mattered. I no longer felt the need to prove myself through metrics that were ultimately meaningless. Instead, I began to measure success by the quality of my relationships, the depth of my passions, and the sense of purpose I found in each day.

One of the first areas where this shift became evident was in my work. Previously, I had chased brand deals and collaborations that promised visibility and financial gain, even if they didn't align with my values or interests. Now, I was more selective, choosing projects that resonated with me on a deeper level. Whether it was a photography series, a writing project, or a collaboration with a cause I believed in, I only took on work that felt authentic and meaningful. This approach might not have brought the same level of fame or financial reward, but it brought me a satisfaction that was far more valuable.

In redefining success, I also learned to appreciate the smaller, everyday victories. Success wasn't just about achieving grand goals or reaching new heights; it was also about finding joy in the present moment, in the little things that made life rich and meaningful. A quiet morning spent with a good book, a conversation with a friend, a creative project that brought me fulfillment—these were the moments that now defined my success. They might not have been flashy or impressive by conventional standards, but they were the things that made me feel truly alive.

This new definition of success also influenced my relationships. In the past, I had often surrounded myself with people who could help me climb the social ladder, who could boost my visibility or provide opportunities. But as I shifted my focus, I began to prioritize relationships that were based on mutual respect, trust, and shared values. Success in this context meant having a circle of friends and loved ones who supported me for who I was, not for what I could offer them. These relationships brought a sense of belonging and connection that was far more rewarding than any number of followers could ever be.

As I embraced this new perspective, I also noticed a change in my sense of purpose. Success was no longer about achieving external goals or meeting societal expectations; it was about living a life that was aligned with my values, passions, and beliefs. This shift allowed me to pursue the things that truly mattered to me, whether they were big or small, popular or obscure. It gave me the freedom to explore new interests, to take risks, and to follow my curiosity without worrying about how it would be perceived by others.

In redefining success, I also learned to let go of the fear of failure. When success was measured by external validation, failure had always seemed like something to be avoided at all costs. But now, I understood that failure was simply a part of the journey, a necessary step in the process of growth and self-discovery. It wasn't something to be feared or ashamed of, but something to learn from and embrace. This realization gave me the courage to try new things, to experiment, and to push myself beyond my comfort zone.

Ultimately, this redefinition of success was about finding balance and harmony in my life. It was about creating a life that was meaningful and fulfilling, not according to someone else's standards, but according to my own. It was about prioritizing the things that brought me joy, that made me feel connected and purposeful, and that allowed me to live in alignment with my true self.

As I settled into this new understanding of success, I felt a sense of peace that I hadn't known was possible. I no longer felt the pressure to constantly achieve, to be seen, or to prove myself. Instead, I was content with the life I was building, one that was rich in relationships, passions, and a sense of purpose. This new definition of success was my own, and it allowed me to live a life that was not only fulfilling but also deeply, authentically mine.

32
Giving Back

As I continued to embrace my redefined version of success, I found myself driven by a new sense of purpose—one that went beyond personal fulfillment. The more I reflected on my journey, the more I realized that the lessons I had learned, the struggles I had overcome, and the growth I had experienced weren't just for me. They were meant to be shared, to inspire and uplift others who might be facing the same challenges. And so, with a renewed sense of direction, I set out to use my platform in a way that truly mattered.

The first step was deciding where to focus my efforts. I knew that I wanted to raise awareness about the issues that had been central to my own transformation—mental health, digital wellness, and the importance of real-life connections. These were areas where I had struggled, where I had seen the darkest parts of myself, and where I had ultimately found healing. I wanted to help others navigate these challenges, to provide them with the tools and support they needed to find their own path to wellness.

But I also knew that I couldn't do this alone. So, I reached out to organizations and experts who were already doing incredible work in these areas. I began to collaborate with mental health advocates, digital detox programs, and community groups that promoted offline connections. These partnerships allowed me to amplify my message and connect with people who could benefit from my story. It wasn't just about speaking out—it was about creating tangible change and offering resources to those who needed them most.

One of the first initiatives I launched was a digital wellness campaign. Using my platform, I encouraged my followers to take a step back from social media, even if just for a day, to experience the world outside of their screens. I shared tips on how to manage screen time, how to set boundaries, and how to rediscover the joys of offline life. The response was overwhelming. Messages poured in from people who had taken the challenge, sharing how it had changed their perspective, how it had brought them closer to their loved ones, or how it had simply given them a much-needed break from the constant noise of the digital world.

This campaign was just the beginning. I also started a series of live talks and online workshops focused on mental health. I spoke openly about my own struggles with anxiety, depression, and the pressures of maintaining a perfect online persona. These sessions weren't about offering quick fixes but about fostering honest conversations and creating a safe space where people could share their experiences. I brought in mental health professionals to provide expert advice, and together, we built a community of support and understanding.

As I continued this work, I began to notice a shift in the way people interacted with me online. The superficial adoration that had once dominated my feed was replaced by something deeper, more genuine. People were reaching out not to praise my appearance or my lifestyle, but to thank me for the impact I was having on their lives. They shared stories of how they had started prioritizing their mental health, how they had reconnected with old friends, or how they had found the courage to step away from toxic digital spaces. These messages touched me in a way that no amount of likes or followers ever could. I realized that this was the kind of influence I had always wanted to have—the kind that made a real difference.

But the most rewarding part of this journey was the way it allowed me to reconnect with my own humanity. In giving back, I found that I was also healing the parts of myself that had been broken by the pressures of my former life. Every time I shared my story, every time I offered support or guidance, I felt a little more whole, a little more grounded in the person I had become. The act of helping others was, in many ways, helping me to continue growing, to continue moving forward on my own path.

One of the most powerful experiences came when I decided to host an offline event—a gathering where people could come together in person, away from their screens, to connect on a human level. The event was simple: a day spent in nature, with activities that encouraged conversation, reflection, and mindfulness. It was a risk, stepping out from behind the safety of the digital world, but it was a risk that paid off in ways I hadn't anticipated. The event was a success, not because of the number of attendees, but because of the connections that were made, the stories that were shared, and the sense of community that emerged. It was a reminder that the most meaningful interactions often happen face-to-face, in the quiet moments when we are truly present with one another.

As my platform continued to evolve, I made it a point to keep my focus on the causes that mattered most to me. I worked to raise funds for mental health organizations, to support initiatives that promoted digital wellness, and to advocate for the importance of real-life connections in an increasingly disconnected world. My influence had taken on a new direction—one that wasn't about me, but about the impact I could have on others. And that was a kind of success that I had never experienced before.

Looking back, I realized how far I had come from the person I used to be. The old me had been consumed by the need for validation, by the desire to be seen and admired. But the new me had found a deeper, more enduring sense of purpose. I had learned that true success wasn't about what I could achieve for myself, but about what I could give back to the world. And in giving back, I had found a fulfillment that was richer and more meaningful than anything I had ever known.

This chapter of my life was one of transformation, not just in how I defined success, but in how I lived it. It was about stepping into a role that allowed me to make a difference, to use my voice for something greater than myself. And in doing so, I had discovered the true power of influence—not as a means of gaining recognition, but as a way of creating lasting, positive change.

33

The Power of Influence

As I looked back on my journey, I realized that the concept of influence had taken on a new meaning for me. There was a time when influence was all about numbers—followers, likes, and the reach of my posts. It was a currency in the digital world, a measure of success that I had once chased relentlessly. But as my life shifted, so did my understanding of what it truly meant to be influential.

Influence, I discovered, wasn't about how many people were watching—it was about the impact I could have on those who were. It was about using my voice to inspire change, to encourage others to live authentically, and to remind them of the importance of balance in a world that often glorified extremes. This realization transformed the way I approached my platform, and it gave me a renewed sense of purpose.

I began to focus on the quality of my message rather than the quantity of my audience. I shared stories of my own struggles and triumphs, hoping that they might resonate with someone else who was facing similar challenges. I spoke openly about the importance of mental health, about the value of stepping away from the digital noise to reconnect with what truly mattered. I encouraged my followers to seek balance, to prioritize their well-being over the pursuit of online validation, and to find fulfillment in real-life connections.

The response was both humbling and inspiring. People began to reach out, sharing their own stories of how they had been influenced by my journey. They spoke of finding the courage to step away from toxic digital spaces, of rediscovering passions they had once abandoned, and of forging deeper, more meaningful relationships. These messages reminded me of the true power of influence—not as a tool for self-promotion, but as a way to uplift and empower others.

In this chapter of my life, I found a deeper sense of fulfillment than I had ever known. It was no longer about being seen or admired, but about making a difference in the lives of others. My influence was measured not by the numbers on a screen, but by the positive change I could inspire. And in helping others find their own path to authenticity and balance, I found a purpose that was richer and more enduring than anything I had ever imagined.

As I continued to use my voice to advocate for what truly mattered, I felt a sense of peace and contentment that had once seemed elusive. I knew that I was on the right path, one that was aligned with my values and my true self. Influence had taken on a new, more profound meaning—one that was not about fame, but about impact. And in embracing this new understanding, I had finally found the fulfillment I had been searching for all along.

34

The Journey Continues

As I stood at the edge of this new beginning, I felt a surge of excitement. Life, with all its unpredictability, had become a thrilling adventure rather than a daunting challenge. I had come a long way, but the best part was knowing that the journey was far from over. Each day offered a fresh start, a new opportunity to grow, learn, and laugh—a lot more than I used to.

The younger me would've scoffed at the idea of finding joy in something as simple as a quiet morning walk or a deep conversation with a friend. Back then, I thought happiness came with a hashtag. But now, I knew better. True fulfillment was about the little things—the genuine moments that made life rich and vibrant. And the best part? You didn't need a filter to make them shine.

Looking ahead, I felt optimistic about the future. I had found a balance that worked for me, and I was eager to share that message with others—especially the younger generation, who are often caught in the same digital whirlwind that had once swept me off my feet. I wanted them to know that it's okay to step back, to take a breath, and to remember that life is happening right here, right now, outside the screen.

To anyone feeling the pressure to be perfect online, here's a little secret: nobody is. Embrace your quirks, laugh at your mistakes, and don't be afraid to log off and live a little. After all, life's too short to waste worrying about the number of likes on your last post. Besides, real friends don't care about your follower count—they care if you'll share your fries.

And for those who think they can't survive a day without checking their feed, remember: if a tree falls in the forest and no one's around to tweet about it, it still makes a sound. The world keeps turning, and it's full of amazing experiences just waiting for you to unplug and enjoy them.

As I moved forward, I was filled with a sense of peace and a hope that others might find their own path to a more balanced, authentic life. The journey is ongoing, and that's what makes it beautiful. So here's to the next adventure, to living with purpose, and to never forgetting that the best stories often happen when we're not looking at our phones.

And if all else fails, remember this: when life gets too serious, a good meme can still save the day.

[PK signs out here ! Go get your dreams ! Get out of this 2GB Ki Zindagi]